Praise for **PHILIP R. CRAIG's**
MARTHA'S VINEYARD MYSTERIES

"Craig just keeps getting better."
Chattanooga Times

"Reading his books is like a pleasant holiday, visiting
old friends (his recurring characters) and enjoying a
popular resort area, all without leaving the comfort
of your favorite chair."
Los Angeles Daily News

"The Martha's Vineyard mysteries are a breath of
fresh air with a touch of murder most foul."
Denver Rocky Mountain News

"[J.W. Jackson's] a marvelous extension of John D. MacDonald's
Travis McGee and maybe even Don Quixote."
Florida Times-Union

"This insinuatingly attractive series, starring J.W.
and Zee Jackson, grows and deepens."
Booklist

"Jackson is smart and tough and believable."
Cleveland Plain Dealer

VINEYARD ENIGMA

A MARTHA'S VINEYARD MYSTERY

PHILIP R. CRAIG

AVON BOOKS
An Imprint of HarperCollinsPublishers

This is a work of fiction. Names, characters, places, and incidents are products of the author's imagination or are used fictitiously and are not to be construed as real. Any resemblance to actual events, locales, organizations, or persons, living or dead, is entirely coincidental.

AVON BOOKS
An Imprint of HarperCollins*Publishers*
10 East 53rd Street
New York, New York 10022-5299

Copyright © 2002 by Philip R. Craig
Published by arrangement with Charles Scribner's Sons
ISBN: 0-06-051188-5
www.avonmystery.com

First Avon Books paperback printing: May 2003

Avon Trademark Reg. U.S. Pat. Off. and in Other Countries,
Marca Registrada, Hecho en U.S.A.
HarperCollins® is a trademark of HarperCollins Publishers Inc.

Printed in the U.S.A.

10 9 8 7 6 5 4 3 2 1

For my son-in-law,
Bill Lynch,
and for my granddaughter,
Bailey Quinn Leone Lynch.

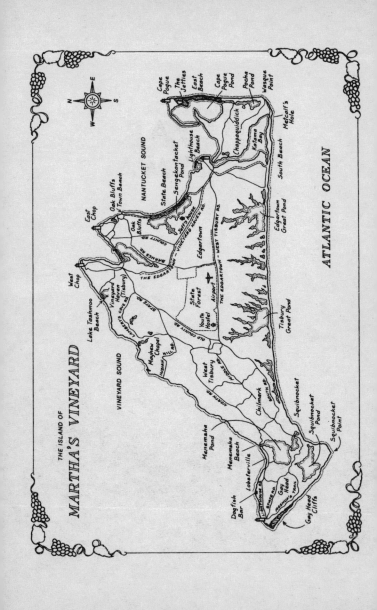

VINEYARD
ENIGMA

Now at the last gasp of love's latest breath,
When, his pulse failing, passion speechless lies,
When faith is kneeling by his bed of death,
And innocence is closing up his eyes,
Now if thou wouldst, when all have given him over
From death to life thou might'st him yet recover.

—MICHAEL DRAYTON

— 1 —

Later I figured I got involved, and almost killed, for three reasons: the money, the case itself, and Zee's uncharacteristic detachment from the world we shared.

If you live on Martha's Vineyard you can always use more money, and the job interested me because it concerned works of art whose history caught my fancy. Most of all, though, I probably agreed to work for Mahsimba because, during an especially warm and lovely spring, Zee had become curiously spell-bound and ethereal, like a teenaged girl.

Her dreaminess had continued on into June and had disconnected her from our normal family life. She was as efficient as ever at her work in the emergency room at the hospital, but she seemed lost in obscure thoughts when at home with the children and me, as though she were seeing the world with the eyes of one who had once been blind.

I had several thoughts about the cause of this, none having anything to do with the others. Perhaps she had relapsed into guilt over killing a Boston thug the year before, even though she'd done it to save herself and our daughter and had taken a gun-shot in the process. Or maybe it was a sort of sustained spring fever. Or maybe she was experiencing some form of the seven-year itch. That wouldn't be too surprising, considering my own certainty of my limitations as a husband. But when I asked her the cause of her sea change, she only pressed her forefinger to my lips and wordlessly shook her head.

Whatever the cause of her enchantment, there seemed to be nothing I could do about it, so I determined to remain unchanged myself, to stay the man whose love had once given her joy, and to hope that it still did or would again, however dreamily removed from me she seemed to be for the nonce. When Mahsimba came into my life I was glad to accept a job that would oblige me to think of something else.

Before the phone rang, I was alone in the house. Zee was at work, the kids were in school, and the cats were off catting somewhere outside. I was finishing my morning coffee and reading the *Vineyard Gazette*'s sixth-months-later story about the Headless Horseman.

That still-unidentified body had long since been placed in some mainland morgue or grave, but on the Vineyard its notoriety had lessened only slightly since the previous December, when an understandably shocked pony rider had discovered it beside a frosty bridle path up in West Tisbury. The equestrian connection explained half of the corpse's nickname, and its missing head accounted for the other half. It could have been called the Handless Horseman, for that matter, because the hands were missing, too, along with the corpse's clothes.

Naked, headless, and handless corpses are not common on Martha's Vineyard, especially in the dead of winter, so locally the discovery had caused quite a stir. Speculation swirled about who had died and why and who had done the deed, and there was much conjecture that someone with a horse was involved since that was clearly how the body had been transported along the trail. Unfortunately for the police, there are many horses and riders on the island and not one of them seemed the type to kill and behead people.

The how was easier; the man, white and in his forties, according to medical reports, had been shot right in the pump with what appeared to be a .38- or .40-caliber bullet. Before this happened, he had apparently been in good physical condition, but that was about all anyone had learned about him. He didn't fit any of the missing person reports that the police had received, and now, half a year later, he was as unknown as ever.

The *Gazette* report, consistent with that famous newspaper's policy of not emphasizing the island's darker side, was short and on a middle page, and contented itself with a brief review of the facts and of the questions that people still talked about: Who was the guy and who had killed him and why?

These questions continued to bother those of the island's citizens who didn't like the idea that they might be sharing their beloved Vineyard with a killer. I, however, was not one of the worriers, because it had been a long time since I'd thought that my island home actually was akin to Eden before the Fall. My Vineyard, for all its fabled loveliness, had its share of snakes living under the rocks.

But I had not moved to the island to get involved with such creatures. I had done enough of that during five years on the Boston PD. The bullet I still carried next to my spine as a consequence of wearing a shield had only been the last factor that led me to decide to let somebody else save the world. I had better things to do.

That very day, for example, I had veggie and flower gardens to tend, floors to vacuum, supper to prepare, a leak in my waders that I had to find and patch, another leak in the ceiling of the porch that I had to track down and fix, clothes to wash, shopping to do, and, most important, fishing to attend to. For the bluefish had been in for a couple of weeks, and I still had more of them to catch.

Ordinarily I could think of little that was more pleasurable than being on the beach doing battle with the blues, and this year fishing was doubly appealing because it also served to distract me from fretting about Zee.

I was just beginning to fret some more when Stanley Crandel phoned.

"J.W., that you?"

"Stanley, where are you? Up at the house?"

"No. London. Just got here from Africa. Went from Cape Town to Cairo. Terrific trip! That's what I'm calling about. Met this man in Harare. Interesting fellow. Seems he's going to the Vineyard. I wonder if you'll show him around, help him out."

"When's he coming?"

"He may be there already. I put him in touch with John Skye, and he'll be staying at John's place because Betsy and I won't get down to our place until later."

"What's he need me for?"

"It's a long story, and this call's costing me a fortune. He'll explain it when he sees you. Will you meet him?"

"Well . . ."

"You'll be doing me a favor."

I hate it when people say that. "All right," I said.

"I knew I could depend on you, J.W. I told him to call you from John's house when he gets in. His name's Mahsimba. Thanks. Gotta go."

The phone clicked and buzzed in my ear.

I shook my head at the thought of a phone call being too expensive for Stanley Crandel to bear. Stanley and his wife, Betsy, owned one of the biggest houses on East Chop, where Crandels had been summering for a hundred years. Stanley liked to think that he was a descendant of John Saunders, the onetime Virginia slave who, some said, was later the first Methodist preacher on the Vineyard. But it had been a long time since Stanley's line of Crandels had been slaves to anything but high finance.

This fact notwithstanding, it was typical of Stanley and Betsy simultaneously to be generous to friends, family, and charities, and yet to squeeze their pennies till they screamed. Maybe they had so many pennies precisely because they pinched them so hard. Maybe that was true of all wealthy people, including the other aristocratic and upper-middle-class African-American citizens of Oak Bluffs. I wouldn't know, being an outsider to such social circles.

I knew Stanley and Betsy because I opened their house in the spring, closed it again in the fall, and looked after it all year long. I'd gotten the job because Stanley and John Skye had gone to college together and John had given Stanley my name. I also opened and closed John's place and cared for it while he and his family were up in Weststock during the winter, where he professed things medieval at the college. I tended to other houses, too, because when you have no steady job, you have to be willing to do a lot of things.

And now, apparently, I was going to have yet another bit of work: showing Mr. Mahsimba around the Vineyard and helping him achieve whatever he had in mind.

I thought of John Skye and his family, and was glad I'd gotten the farm ready for their arrival. The twins were now in college, so they'd be getting out of school at the same time as their father did. Thus, all of the Skyes might be descending from America any day now. I presumed that John would arrive before Mr. Mahsimba did. I wondered what Mr. Mahsimba's long story would be, but there was no way to guess.

I went back to perusing the *Gazette*. Since I'd taken the phone call, the Headless Horseman was still unidentified, and the case was still open as unsolved murder cases always are. I thought about the Woman in the Dunes, over on Cape Cod. There were similarities between her case and that of the Horseman. The woman's handless body had been found years before in the sand dunes, her jeans folded neatly beside her. She was still unidentified after many years. A very cold case, but one that was still open.

The latest effort at identifying her involved opening the grave and attempting DNA tests, which hadn't been available when she'd first been found. I imagined that DNA evidence had also been taken from the Horseman, but that nothing had been done with it because of the absence of comparable samples.

I put the paper down, stopped thinking about crime, finished my coffee, and considered the many things that needed doing. An old guy once told me that the good part about being retired is that you still have lots of things to do but you don't have to do them. I wasn't quite retired, so I still had to do them, but I had some choices about when and in which order.

So I went fishing.

It was still early enough in the season for Norton Point Beach to be open, so I went that way, over the sand from Katama toward Chappy. Soon impassioned Department of Fish and Wildlife agents would close Norton Point to ORV traffic on the grounds that passing trucks disturbed nesting and fledging plovers. It was one of those governmental decisions that explains anarchism, since the real threats to plovers, as even the beach-closers knew, were gulls, skunks, and other wild predators. Maddening. When I'm king, I'm shipping all of the plovers and environmentalists to No Man's Land, where they can care for one another and not bother the rest of us. The world will thank me for it.

I stopped here and there and made casts into the light southwest wind. I caught nothing, but that was okay, because it was a lovely early June day, with bright sun and a clear light blue sky arching down and meeting the dark blue ocean on the southern horizon. If you sailed that way, the first land you'd come to would be Hispaniola, which was well beyond my longest cast.

I fished awhile at Metcalf's Hole and got one lone five-pound blue which apparently had no friends. I cut his throat, rinsed him off, and put him on the ice in the fish box, then went on to Wasque.

Wasque Point is the southeastern corner of Chappaquiddick, the peninsula hooked to the rest of the Vineyard by Norton Point Beach. When the water broke through the beach between the ocean and Katama Bay, Chappy became an island and remained one until Neptune in his wisdom closed the opening again. Wasque is one of the best places in the world to catch bluefish, because of the tides that form the Wasque rip, where bait is tossed about and the blues go after it. When conditions are right you can slaughter the blues at Wasque.

They weren't perfect that morning, but they were good enough, and the surf casters who were stretched in a line along the beach in front of their four-by-fours were busy and happy. I became one of them, and when I finally broke off and went home, the blues were still there, hitting almost anything you threw, filling the air with the scent of watermelon.

In town I sold all of my fish but one and took that one home. On the filleting table behind our shed I scaled and filleted the fish and then took the fillets into the house and put them in the fridge. We'd have stuffed bluefish for supper. Delish! My mouth was already watering.

It was a little past noon and I was having my first Sam Adams of the day when the phone rang again.

John Skye's voice was on the other end. "The groves of academe have shed the Skyes for another summer," said John. "We're here."

"If I'd known that a little earlier, I'd have brought you a bluefish."

"I can catch my own bluefish, thanks. Are you busy right now?"

"I'm drinking a beer, but it won't take long to finish it."

"Fine. Come on over. There's someone I want you to meet. His name is Mahsimba."

— 2 —

John Skye owned a farm off the West Tisbury road, complete with barn, outbuildings, and a corral. He and Mattie and their twin daughters summered there when they weren't in Colorado, where John had grown up.

The girls were two of the island's many horse people. They rode Eastern when on the Vineyard and Western when out on the old Skye place on the Florida Mesa, south of Durango. John had been smart enough early on to buy the Vineyard farm even though his limited professorial salary made the purchase much beyond his means. He had pinched and borrowed and gone without for years before inflation and his improving income transformed the farm into an unbelievably great bargain.

It was the reverse of a more common Vineyard tale, which turned on the theme of "I could have bought such and such a piece of land for five hundred dollars, but back then I didn't have five hundred dollars, so I didn't buy it, and look at the price of it now!"

I was the beneficiary of a tale like John's. My father, before I was born, had bought the place where Zee and I now lived. At that time it was land nobody wanted, so he'd bought as much as his fireman's wages allowed and now the place was mine and, like

John's farm, the object of many a developer's eye. Someday, if I got hungry enough, I might sell a piece of it. But not yet.

I drove up our long sandy driveway, took a left on the paved road, and went into Edgartown. It was still early in June but already the giant seasonal A & P/Al's Package Store traffic jam was in evidence. Later, during the height of summer, it would clog the road for half a mile in each direction, thanks to people trying to make left turns for food or booze. When I'm king of the world, I'm banning all left turns.

I slipped smoothly on down past Cannonball Park, took a right on the West Tisbury Road, and was soon pulling into John's driveway. There, I parked in front of his big white house, waved at a twin with a horse down by the barn, and knocked on the front door.

Mattie opened it and gave me a hug and a kiss. "The place looks fine, J.W. You even got that sticky window in the kitchen to slide up and down. Come on in. John's in the library."

"You look great," I said, leering. "If I wasn't married already, I'd propose."

"And if I wasn't married and didn't know you as well as I do, I might accept." She waved toward the library. "Go on in. They're waiting for you." She leaned forward and whispered, "Mahsimba is a hunk!"

Hunkiness is a quality best understood by women, so I wasn't as enlightened by the remark as Zee might have been. It was, I knew, a statement of physical and psychosexual approval, but why some men were hunks and others weren't was a mystery to me.

John Skye's library was a large room with ceiling-high shelves filled with thousands of books. It was furnished with leather chairs, reading lamps, and Oriental carpets. Against one wall was the huge, ancient, carved table that John used as a desk. It was piled with books and papers and held a computer, printer, and scanner. Above the desk, high on the wall, hung a battered fencing mask centering a rusty triangulation of épée, saber, and foil, tokens of John's long-ago collegiate career as a three-weapon man.

It was one of the finest rooms I knew, and when opening or closing the house for the season, I often got distracted there and only later realized I was reading instead of working, in the thrall of books.

John and another man were bent over the desk, looking at a book. They straightened and turned as I came in.

John, tall, lean, and the possessor of a slight potbelly of which he was unashamed ("security rations in case of atomic attack"), smiled and met me in the middle of the room. "J.W. Good to see you."

I took his hand and nodded toward the desk. "Still at work on *Gawain*, I take it."

"If *Beowulf* can become a bestseller, *Gawain* can, too. Fame and wealth will at last be mine."

John had been working on a definitive translation of *Gawain and the Green Knight* for as long as I could remember. Recently a translation of *Beowulf*, another epic usually read only by English majors, and reluctantly at that, had, to the astonishment and delight of medievalists, made the top ten on the *New York Times* bestseller list.

John turned. "Let me introduce you two. Mahsimba, this is J. W. Jackson, the man Stan Crandel told you about. J.W., this is Abraham Mahsimba."

Our hands met. His grip was both gentle and sinewy.

"How do you do, Mr. Jackson?"

"My friends call me J.W."

He smiled. "And I am called Mahsimba. I have other names, but most people find them long and unpronounceable."

"Mahsimba it is, then."

"And J.W. it is."

Mahsimba was of medium height and looked to be about a middleweight. His skin was smooth and the color of coffee with a tablespoon of cream. His hair was short, dark, and lay close to his skull, and his eyes were golden brown. He had high cheekbones, and his nose was slightly curved beneath a high, clear brow. His teeth, as he smiled, were white and flawless. He was wearing canvas and leather shoes and casual clothing that could have come from anywhere. A curious ivory carving hung on a gold chain around his neck.

"Stan Crandel put me in touch with Mahsimba here," said John, "and Stan and I both think that you might be just the guy to help him out."

I nodded. "Stanley said as much, but he didn't say how. Just that it was a long story."

John waved us all to leather chairs. "It's the medieval connection that's got me interested," he said. "But it's your story, Mahsimba, so I'll shut up."

Mahsimba nodded and turned to me. "Are you familiar with the history of Africa?"

"I know about Egypt and the pyramids, and I know there are diamond mines down south. I've read that the Queen of Sheba may have come from there, and I've seen movies about Tarzan, King

Solomon's mines, and the Zulu wars. But that's about it."

"Unfortunately, many Africans know less than that. I am searching for two stone birds." He paused, then saw something in my face that made him smile. "No, neither of them is the Maltese falcon. I leave the search for that black bird to others, though the birds I seek are also works of art. They are fish eagles carved from soapstone perhaps seven hundred years ago. Are you familiar with the ruins now called Great Zimbabwe?"

I thought back. "A very large, very old circular stone enclosure with some sort of tower inside it? I remember reading about it and seeing some photos. In *National Geographic,* maybe. It was a while back."

"Your memory is correct. When I was a child, my village was in what was then Rhodesia but is now Zimbabwe. The ruins were not far away, and I visited them from time to time.

"The original structures were built between 1100 and 1500 A.D. and were part of the principal city of the kingdom of Monomotapa. For four hundred years its citizens raised cattle and mined gold, copper, and iron. By 1500 they were trading with Arabs and the Portuguese, who came inland from the east coast.

"Then Monomotapa declined and was forgotten by the outside world until its rediscovery by Europeans in the nineteenth century. A German, Carl Mauch, visited the ruins in 1871 and speculated that the buildings had been erected by the Phoenicians."

Here Mahsimba allowed himself a wry smile. "It is an interesting footnote to African history and politics that as recently as the 1970s it was illegal in Rhodesia for any official document to advance the thesis that Great Zimbabwe had been built by black Africans. Egyptians were a more acceptable explanation, or a lost tribe of Israel."

I thought of how the Nazis' refusal to use what they called "Jewish science" may have caused them the loss of a war they perhaps could have won. Racism is an odd and often self-destructive vice.

"In any case," continued Mahsimba, "with the discovery of the ruins came European treasure hunters and so-called experts on ancient cultures. One of the treasure hunters was a man named Willi Posselt. In 1889 he discovered four eagles carved from soapstone and traded for what he considered the best of them. Over the years, a total of ten eagles were found in Great Zimbabwe and shipped elsewhere, to museums and private collections. The whereabouts of eight of them are known, and my country is working very hard to have them returned to their homeland. I'm here on your island in search of the two missing ones. I think they may be here, and Stanley Crandel thinks that you may be able to help me find them."

— 3 —

John leaned forward. "Stan Crandel and I both think you're the guy for the job, J.W. You were a cop and you know the island as well as anyone and better than most."

I said nothing.

"If it's a matter of money," said Mahsimba, misreading my silence, "I have been authorized to spend whatever is reasonable to find the birds, and I will be pleased to employ you at a figure that is agreeable to us both." He mentioned a sum that was very agreeable indeed.

"That's a fair amount of money," I said.

"You may earn it, if you accept the work. There is an element of danger in the job. Millions of dollars are being made in the international art trade, and many people who are not scrupulous are involved in the illegal aspect of it. Those people can be quite dangerous, and some of them might be right here on your lovely island."

"I don't mind a little trouble," I said, "but I'm not sure I can be of help to you. I know nothing at all about the illegal art trade, other than that a lot of people make a lot of money at it, and I only know two people who've been to southern Africa or know anything about the art that comes from there."

"Vineyarders travel all the time," said John. "I'll bet dozens of them have been to Africa."

"Who are the two people you mentioned?" asked Mahsimba.

"Al Butters is a retired guy who spends all summer sailing," I said. "I met him because we both have cat-boats about the same size, and we both go out and float around in the annual catboat race. He worked for some outfit that sent him and Barbara to south-ern Africa for five or six years. Now they have a house here full of African baskets and carvings. But I've never seen anything there that looks like a soap-stone eagle."

Mahsimba's eyes looked into mine. "When was he working in Africa?"

"I'm not sure. I think he retired about five years ago."

"Ah. The eagles disappeared years before that."

"But it's a place to start, J.W.," said John. "Go talk with Al Butters. Maybe he knows somebody who has a couple of stone eagles."

I could feel temptation tugging at me. I wanted distraction, even at the risk of some degree of danger.

"I don't think you need to know too much about art," said John. "This island is crawling with artists and people involved with galleries, museums, and the like. You can tap their brains if you need to know more than you already do. What Mahsimba needs is someone who knows his way around this island and who has some experience asking questions."

"I only hope the Zimbabwe eagles are actually here," said Mahsimba, raising a cautionary hand. "It has been a hundred years since their existence was first reported, and the two I seek have not been publicly seen since then."

"But you're here," I said, "on this particular dot in the water, eight thousand miles from your home country. You didn't come here just by chance."

"Very true." Mahsimba took a small notebook from his shirt pocket, opened it, and scanned several pages. My impression, however, was that he knew the contents so well that his reading was not really necessary. "During the 1960s, an American adventurer named Ronald Parsons was in Rhodesia, working as a mercenary in one of the irregular units the Ian Smith government was employing to combat the revolutionaries.

"Foreseeing earlier than most that the white government was not going to prevail, Parsons took what he could find in the way of loot, which was considerable, and departed. Included in his booty were two stone Zimbabwe eagles taken from the farm of an Englishman whose grandfather had been a cohort of Cecil Rhodes himself.

"These birds were ornately carved and had originally been part of the grandfather's private collections. Eventually, they became the property of his grandson, Crompton, who owned the farm from which Parsons took them. The Crompton family diaries and journals make reference to the carved birds, and some contain photos of them. Here is one of those photos. Keep it."

I looked down at a none-too-clear photo of a collection of baskets and wood carvings in the center of which were two pale stone stelae ornamented with what appeared to be carved crocodiles and topped

with sculpted hawks or eagles. I looked back at
Mahsimba.

"And Parsons brought these birds to America?"

"Yes. Our organization eventually traced him to
California. Last November David Brownington, one
of several agents hired to find the birds, went there
to talk with him. But many years had passed, and
Parsons had fallen on hard times and had sold the
birds to a private collector specializing in Africana.
Parsons would not give his name. However, a woman
who had been hired by Parsons to help write his
memoirs, but who had then had a falling-out with
him, was eager to take what revenge she could. She
learned of Brownington's interview with Parsons,
contacted him, and gave him the name of the dealer
who had arranged the sale of the birds, a Daniel
Duarte. Is the name familiar to you?"

"There are a lot of Duartes on this island, but I
don't know of any named Daniel. Should I?"

"Daniel Duarte was born on Martha's Vineyard
but had been living for many years in San Francisco, where his firm was located, so Brownington
went there. Although he was unable to persuade
Duarte to reveal the name of the buyer of the birds,
Brownington did learn that Duarte's son, Matthew,
who is a junior partner in the firm, manages a
branch of the family business here. His office is on
the old family farm, in a town called West Tisbury.
Have you heard of this Matthew Duarte?"

"I may have heard the name, but I don't know the
man. Fourteen thousand people live on the Vineyard, and I don't know most of them."

"Very understandable. In any case, Brownington
learned that Matthew Duarte might have been

involved in the sale of the birds and so informed his principals. Nothing has been heard from Brownington since."

Mahsimba's golden eyes were fathomless. "Other matters kept me occupied for several months, but now I've been given the task of finding the birds. I sent a message to Matthew Duarte's Web site and told him I was coming here in hopes of interviewing him. If that interview proves unhelpful and if other efforts to find the birds here fail, I'll go on to San Francisco to try to trace them from there."

"You must want them pretty badly."

"They are worth a fortune to collectors, and middlemen and dealers can therefore make small fortunes of their own by arranging their sale and delivery. But they are priceless symbols to my country, and we want them back."

"Describe Brownington," I said.

Mahsimba raised a brow. "Describe David Brownington? David is in his early forties, about six feet tall, very fit, blond, a Zimbabwean of British descent whose people have been in Africa for generations. Well educated, well spoken. A very able fellow. We met at Oxford." He tipped his head slightly to one side as he stared at something he saw in my face. "Why do you ask?"

"Because David Brownington may be dead." I told him about the Headless Horseman. "Brownington dropped out of sight in California about the time the Horseman's body was discovered. If Brownington came here to interview Matthew Duarte, chances are the authorities knew nothing about it, so they'd have no reason to link this body to a foreigner last seen three thousand miles away."

Mahsimba frowned. "David Brownington is not the sort of man who's easy to kill."

"Tough people get killed when they least expect it," I said, thinking of the gunman Zee had shot.

Mahsimba nodded. "That is true. I'm more eager than ever to talk to Mr. Matthew Duarte."

"If Brownington actually is the Horseman," I said, "it doesn't mean that Duarte killed him. Someone else may have wanted to keep Brownington from talking to Duarte and may have stopped him before they met."

"And who might that have been?"

"It could have been someone who didn't want Brownington to learn the name of the person who bought the birds. Maybe it was the buyer himself."

Mahsimba drummed his fingers on the arm of his chair. "How would he have known Brownington was coming?"

"Duarte might have told him. Or Duarte might have told someone else, who then told the killer."

John, whose profession made him reluctant to jump to conclusions, frowned. "I think this is all a stretch," he said, "but maybe we should contact the police and put this bug in their ear."

Mahsimba's face was without emotion, but his fingers continued to tap lightly against his chair while John rose and went to the phone.

I thought for a moment, then got up and followed John to his desk, where I found and opened the Martha's Vineyard telephone book.

There, listed for all to see, was the name and address of Matthew Duarte, dealer in art and antiques.

John took the phone from his ear. "The police would like to talk with you, Mahsimba. They're interested in anything you can tell them about David Brownington."

Mahsimba nodded. "Of course." He rose as John spoke again into the phone and hung up. Then the three of us climbed into my truck and drove to the Edgartown police station.

The chief was in his office. He looked at me. "You, of course. I should have known you'd be involved in this." He shook Mahsimba's hand. "Sit down, Mr. Mahsimba, and let me hear what you have to say. John, why don't you and what's-his-name here take a walk so Mr. Mahsimba and I can have some privacy."

I turned toward the door. "You're absolutely sure you don't need me here, Chief?"

"I'm absolutely sure," said the chief.

Outside, John and I leaned against the truck. "Someday you may razz the wrong guy," said John.

I held up two fingers pressed together. "The chief and I are just like that. We're blood brothers."

Half an hour later, Mahsimba came out and we all got into the truck.

"The chief is contacting your state police," said Mahsimba. "They apparently handle all murder investigations."

"I'll tell you what I think," I said. "I think we should go up to West Tisbury and have a chat with Matthew Duarte before some cop or lawyer tells us we can't do that."

John nodded. "Good idea."

"Yes," said Mahsimba.

West Tisbury is set right in the middle of Martha's Vineyard and has always been an agricultural town rather than one devoted to the fruits of the sea. The town center consists of the general store, the town hall, the art gallery with its field full of dancing statues, the library, and not much more. The people who live in West Tisbury think it's the best town on the island and only leave it when they drive to Oak Bluffs or Edgartown to buy liquor. When you're driving the roads of West Tisbury, it's more like being in Vermont than being on an island.

Matthew Duarte's house was off South Road, just before the Chilmark line and not far from the little house where Zee lived before we got married and she moved in with me. The house was one of those old but well-maintained farmhouses that you find all over the island, which once was much devoted to pastures and the raising of sheep. If you look at photos of the Vineyard taken around 1900, you'll see a lot of stone walls, but there's hardly a tree in sight.

We passed through the gateway in Matthew Duarte's stone fence and went along the sandy driveway until we got to the house. There was a car parked in front of a barn that was fronted by both double doors and a single door, over which hung a sign: DUARTE AND SON, DEALERS IN FINE ART AND ANTIQUES. The place had that air of emptiness that you feel when there's nobody home.

We went up onto the porch and I knocked at the door.

Nothing.

I knocked again. More nothing.

"He's probably in the office," said John, and started toward the barn.

I walked a few steps along the porch to a window, where I put my head against the glass and peeked in. There was a body on the floor.

4

The West Tisbury police station, which sits beside the village millpond, is one of the smallest on the island, with barely room for three cars to park in front of it. Maybe this is because West Tisbury has lots less crime than towns with bigger stations. Or maybe not. In any case, the chief in this tiny station is as able as any of the other island police chiefs, of whom there are many, since the Vineyard sports at least ten different police forces.

Just why an island with only fourteen thousand permanent residents needs ten police forces is a mystery to everyone who doesn't live there, and to many who do. Put it down to the same village rivalries that allowed the building of the regional high school only after years of intense argument and invective, some of which continues decades later. There is no more chance of regionalizing the police departments than there is of regionalizing any of the other schools or having a single Vineyard fire department.

In the living room of Matthew Duarte's house, Kate McMillan, chief of the WTPD, studied the body on the floor while waiting for Dom Agganis of the state police to arrive and take over the investigation. If Kate was angry about the law that took murder investigations out of the hands of local cops and gave them to the state guys, she never showed it.

"It's Matt Duarte, all right. Hasn't been dead too long, I'd say." Having ascertained that the corpse was indeed lifeless, she now stepped back, put her strong hands on her strong hips, and studied the room.

John, Mahsimba, and I stood on the porch and looked through the door, taking advantage of the prestige that came with being the discoverers of the body.

"Is that really a bullet hole in the back of his head?" I asked.

"The medical examiner will give us the official info on that," said Kate, "but it sure looks like one to me. No gun in sight, either, so if he committed suicide, I'm damned if I can figure out how he managed it. No, boys, I think we can safely say we've got a possible murder on our hands."

"First the Headless Horseman and now this," I said. "Two murders in a single year is a higher average than usual for Martha's Vineyard."

"Too high," said Kate. She looked at the nervous young summer cop who had arrived with her. "Make sure nobody comes inside until Dom Agganis gets here. I'm going to take a look around."

"Yes, ma'am," said the young cop. He crossed his arms and stood in the door.

Kate moved down a hall, careful not to touch anything, aware of what any detective can tell you: that the police, particularly high officials such as commanders and commissioners who are eager to be seen, corrupt more crime scenes than any other people do.

It was a big house, so Kate might be gone awhile. I touched Mahsimba's shoulder and he followed me down the porch. "When did you e-mail this guy and tell him you were coming?" I asked.

"Two days ago, when I was in London. I had just made my plane reservations, so I knew when I'd be here."

"I believe in coincidences," I said, "but I'm not sure this is one of them. It's possible that Mr. Duarte there told somebody about your message and that somebody didn't want him talking to you."

Mahsimba didn't look the least astonished. "First Brownington and now Duarte himself, eh? If your theory is correct, I would very much like to know to whom he spoke."

I looked in the window through which I'd first seen Matthew Duarte's body. The corpse was right where it had been before. I looked around the room, but nothing caught my eye other than one of those wooden animal carvings that people bring home from Africa. This one was on the fireplace mantel and was a very nice carving of a lion feeding on a dead antelope.

"What do you make of that?" I asked Mahsimba, pointing.

He studied the piece. "It looks like Shona craftsmanship, but I can't be sure. The piece is exceptionally fine."

"It's a link between Matthew Duarte and Africa, at least."

"Yes. And it speaks well of his taste."

From the northeast came the sound of a siren, and not much later a caravan composed of two state patrol cars and one sheriff's-department car came into the yard. Sergeant Dom Agganis and Officer

Olive Otero, followed by Sheriff Peter Blankenship, came up onto the porch.

Olive Otero was carrying a camera. She gave me an irritated look. "You. I should have known you'd be here. Whenever there's trouble, you're in the middle of it."

"Ah, ah," I said, "let's have no verbal abuse from the police, Olive. Like always, I'm innocent as a lamb."

"Can it, you two," said Dom, who had long since grown tired of Olive and me sparring whenever we met. Olive and I had rubbed each other wrong from the start and had never gotten over it. It had been mutual dislike at first sight, the flip side of love. "Go in and take some pictures, Olive."

Olive glared at me and went into the house.

"You three found the body, I hear," said Agganis. "I'll want to talk with you, so stick around." He followed Olive inside.

"You and Olive," said Pete Blankenship, shaking his head. "What a pair." He went into the house.

I left John and Mahsimba on the porch and walked back to the barn.

"Hey," said the young cop, "I don't think you should go down there."

I pretended not to hear him, and looked first at the car and then rattled the office door. It was locked. I walked around to the side of the barn, where there was an office window. I peeked in but didn't see any soapstone eagles or any messages scrawled in blood saying the butler did it.

I went on around the barn and noted that its other windows were boarded up. There were double doors in the back of the barn but they, like the front double doors, were also locked. Security was tight at the Duarte and Son offices.

I walked around the house but saw no evidence that anyone had broken through any windows or the kitchen door. It occurred to me that Mahsimba might be able to read signs that I missed, but I had enough confidence in my own eyes to be fairly sure that whoever had killed Matthew Duarte had come into the house by the front door.

Having seen no indications of struggle in the living room, I was also pretty sure that Duarte had known his killer and had let him or her in. It also seemed that he had trusted the killer enough to turn away and get a bullet in the back of his head. Hadn't something similar happened to Jesse James?

I went back up onto the porch. The young cop looked uncomfortable and annoyed. I'd felt the same way fairly often when I'd been a young cop, so I said, "I didn't touch anything but the office doorknob," and he looked slightly relieved.

The police were inside the house for quite a while before Agganis finally came out. He nodded toward his cruiser and we followed him there. I could feel the eyes of the young cop on our backs as he wished he could hear our conversation.

Agganis got a tape recorder out of the car. "You mind if I use this? If you do, say so and I'll chuck it."

"You want to give us the Miranda first?" I asked.

"No, I don't want to give you the damned Miranda, but I will if you want it. Do you?"

"What is this Miranda?" asked Mahsimba.

We explained. "It's an official warning that if we don't want to say anything, we don't have to until we get ourselves some lawyers to advise us. But if we do talk, what we say can be used as evidence in case the DA decides to charge us with something."

Mahsimba's smile was gone as quick as it came. "I don't think I've been in your country long enough to have committed any major crimes, Officer."

John waved an airy hand. "Miranda us all, Sergeant Agganis. Maybe you can solve this crime right here and now and save yourself and the state a lot of investigation time."

"Fat chance of that," said Agganis. "Even if you confessed this second we'd still have to investigate just to make sure you weren't lying. Perps have more rights than the victims these days." He gave us the Miranda warning and then held up the tape recorder again. "Now, anybody mind if I use this?"

Nobody minded, and Agganis listened to the story of how we happened to find the remains of Matthew Duarte, and to my hypothesis that there might be a relationship between Mahsimba's e-mail and Duarte's death.

Dom, understandably, didn't seem to be too taken with my theory. "This ain't a television show," he said. "Chances are that Duarte got plugged for some simple, down-to-earth reason, like most people. A woman, or money, or dope, or some combination of the three. When we start digging, you can bet we'll find something like that, not anything to do with stolen eagles from Africa. Where can I find you if I need to, Mr. Mahsimba?"

"He's staying with me," said John.

"Until I find the eagles or go west to San Francisco," said Mahsimba.

"And how long will that be?" asked Agganis.

Mahsimba shrugged a small shrug. "The death of

Mr. Duarte makes my work here more complicated and my success more unlikely."

"Well, don't leave without telling me."

Mahsimba gave a slight bow. "I will inform you, Sergeant."

"And I will inform you in the unlikely chance that we stumble across any information about your Zimbabwe eagles. All right, men, I guess we're through here for now. You can get on about your business." Agganis put his tape recorder back into the cruiser and walked into the house.

The three of us drove back to John's farm. There, John said, "J.W., why don't you and Zee come over for dinner tonight? One of the twins can baby-sit the kids at your place."

As any cook will tell you, a meal prepared by someone else is always welcome. My bluefish supper could wait until tomorrow. "Sure," I said, "we'll be glad to."

Much had happened since Stan Crandel's morning call, but there was still a lot of day left before the kids came home from school, so I headed for the Edgartown library. I was glad to be working.

5

Libraries are treasure houses. They are full of books, information, and entertainment, and are manned by people who actually like to help you find what you're looking for. Little in history has caused me more despair about mankind than tales of the destruction of libraries. The ancient desolations of the great archives of Alexandria, Constantinople, and Tenochtitlán fill me with despair and anger whenever I am reminded of them. Not many people are more loathsome in my eyes than book burners.

No such people worked in the Edgartown library, only book lovers, one of whom smiled at me from behind her desk.

"What brings you here on a fine afternoon like this one, J.W.? I'd have guessed you'd be off somewhere fishing."

"I did my fishing this morning. Now I'm in search of other game. Cecil Rhodes, to be precise."

"Cecil Rhodes, is it? Well, go right over there to the computer and you should be able to track him down."

When I was a lad, you tracked library subjects down in the card files, but nowadays card files are only a memory, so I went to the computer and found Cecil there. If the electricity failed, I thought grumpily, nobody would be able to find anything in modern libraries; not that it would make much difference, since the whole world would probably stop spinning.

I spent an hour reading about Cecil, about the origins of Rhodesia, and about the later transformation of Rhodesia into Zambia and Zimbabwe.

Cecil, founder of the Rhodes scholarships and dreamer of the Cape-to-Cairo railway that had never been built, hadn't lived to see fifty, but nevertheless had managed to change the face of southern Africa for a hundred years. His success as an owner of diamond mines made all the difference.

He had been one of those sincere racists who was convinced that Anglo-Saxons were the peak of evolution and the fulfillment of a divine master plan, and he considered it his duty to make sure of the plan's success by extending the British Empire around the world. Part of this grand design, I noted with interest, was a scheme to recover the United States for the Crown, including, presumably, Martha's Vineyard.

He entered the Cape parliament; manipulated boundary commissions; bargained with local African chiefs; persuaded London to oppose German, Belgian, and Boer interests and support his own; negotiated, quarreled, amalgamated with opponents; annexed territory; fomented a revolution; conspired, schemed, survived censure; and otherwise did his best to establish "British dominion from the Cape to Cairo."

His success was considerable, but native revolutionary sentiments, never far beneath the surface of European colonial rule, emerged strongly throughout Africa after World War II, and in the last quarter of the twentieth century, governments organized and run by whites were, one by one, replaced by governments dominated by black Africans. Northern Rhodesia became Zambia and Southern Rhodesia became Zimbabwe, home of Abraham Mahsimba, seeker of the Zimbabwe eagles.

Unfortunately for Africa, its new black leaders were as corrupt and power hungry as the whites they had replaced, and newer revolutionary groups were now seeking to overthrow them in their turn.

Everything changes, nothing changes. Rhodesia had been born out of intrigues, ambitions, schemes, double dealings, and passion, and a hundred years later Zimbabwe was being governed the same way.

I thought about Africa's diamond mines, gold mines, silver mines, and lead mines, about its millions of acres of rich farmland, and about the fortunes made in tourism, industry, communications, and transportation. I thought about the convolutions of African history, and about its politics, which, like the stock market, were driven in such large part by the fear and greed and ancient hatreds so well understood by Machiavelli.

Chinatown.

I found some material on Great Zimbabwe and read that. Like much of Africa, it had been raided, raped, and misunderstood by the unstoppable white migrations that had come north from the Cape in much the same fashion as white Europeans had poured west across America, sweeping all before them. On both continents, Stone Age and Iron Age people had no chance against gunpowder.

I left my reading materials on a table, as librarians prefer their customers to do, so the writings can be put back where they belong instead of elsewhere, and as I passed the desk, the woman sitting at the desk smiled.

"Find what you were looking for, J.W.?"

"I found out where I'm starting from, anyway."

"Come back soon."

"I will."

The young sun shone down on the clean streets of Edgartown, and the strolling early-season tourists looked happy as they window-shopped along the narrow streets and ogled the green lawns and flowers and the great white captains' houses that lined North Water Street. Just across the harbor channel they could look at Chappaquiddick, or, if they were more adventurous, they could take the little three-car On Time ferry to the other side and go biking or driving along the winding Chappy roads.

None of them knew of the body lying not ten miles away in a fine old West Tisbury farmhouse. And I wasn't going to tell them about it.

I got into my truck and went home, so I could be there when the kids got out of school.

I wondered if Zee was still going to be abstracted when she got home from work, and thought old thoughts: Had family life begun to bore her? Had I begun to bore her? Was the wander-thirst upon her? Was her soul in Cathay? Did her fortieth birthday, although still a way in front of her, cast a shadow across her path? Forty had been easy for me, but maybe not even the thought of it was easy for her.

For me, thirty had been the killer birthday, because it meant, somehow, that it was time for me to grow up instead of planning to do it later. Time for me to stop preparing to live and get going on the real thing. I had been depressed for several weeks, because I'd greatly enjoyed being a child.

Maybe Zee was going through something similar. Maybe she was in one of those "there must be more to life than this" moods that can sometimes lead us to either comedy or tragedy.

The cats, Oliver Underfoot and Velcro, welcomed me home. They were in the yard, taking advantage of the late-spring sun. I'd no sooner sat down on the porch steps to have a chat with them when I heard the phone ring. For once I was near enough to the door to avoid the mad dash that I often had to make to get there before the ringing stopped.

Mattie Skye was the caller. "Plans have changed. Bring the kids with you when you come for supper. John will grill burgers and hot dogs. We'll eat early, so your tads can get home to bed in time. Zee and I can catch up on woman things when you men have finished telling us all about finding Matthew Duarte."

"I imagine John and Mahsimba have already told you what there is to tell."

"If a story is worth hearing once, it's worth hearing twice, and, besides, maybe you'll remember something John forgot."

"Not likely."

"Five-thirty?"

"Sounds good."

I hung up feeling hopeful. Maybe Mattie Skye could find out what was causing Zee's mood.

I opened a small can of cat food, divided it into two dishes, and went to the door.

"Snack time!"

The cats, with comforting predictability, came running.

6

Zee was glad to learn of Mattie's invitation, and Joshua and Diana were even more delighted because it was a school night and they were going visiting anyway, and, better yet, because they were going to see the Skye twins, two of their favorite people.

While Zee got out of her working clothes and into her civvies, I leaned against the bedroom door frame and told her about meeting Mahsimba and finding Matthew Duarte's body.

Since Zee was a nurse and worked at the hospital emergency ward, suffering and death were not new to her; still, homicide is always interesting to most people, since they find it almost impossible to imagine why anyone would do such a thing, and Zee was instantly attentive.

"Shot in the head, you say?"

"That's the initial report, anyway."

"When did it happen? Do they know?"

"The medical examiner will give his best guess about that when they ship the body to the mainland. My impression was that he hadn't been dead very long."

"Brrrr. It gives me the creeps to think that we've got a murderer walking around the island."

I knew what she meant, but both of us also knew that the Vineyard had at least its share of criminals.

Anyone who doubted it needed only to hang around the courthouse on Thursdays and listen to the proceedings as lawyers and their clients appeared before the judge. Every week, drug dealers, carousers, thieves, wife beaters, drunk-and-disorderlies, and life's other losers paraded by His Honor. Most, to the disgust of the police, were released onto the streets again to continue their lives of stupidity and petty crime.

We knew, too, that it's sometimes a short step between lesser villainies and larger ones, and that most criminal violence occurs between people who walk on the wild side, so I wasn't surprised when Zee went on to say, "I wonder what Matthew Duarte did to get himself killed. I thought he was one of those proper people who only dealt with other proper people."

"Even art dealers get killed now and then."

"Was he robbed? Did you notice any signs that the house had been burgled?"

"No, but I didn't see much of the inside. Maybe he got shot by a jealous husband."

"Or by his wife or a double-crossed girlfriend. I think I heard that he was a ladies' man. Maybe one of them didn't like being replaced."

"Did you get that from the famous hospital grapevine? What else have you heard about him?"

"Nothing," she said. "We mostly stick to rumors about people doing other people wrong. I was just reading about the Headless Horseman. They don't know who did him in either. Spooky. Do you suppose the same person killed both of them?"

I told her my theory about the Horseman maybe being David Brownington.

"That's a pretty big 'maybe,' Jefferson."

"You're not the only one who thinks so, but I'm not tossing the idea out while it's still warm."

"Well, it would explain some things. But didn't you say Brownington was last heard of out on the West Coast?"

"All I know is what people tell me and what I read in the papers."

"Are you going to work with this Mr. Mahsimba?"

"I haven't really decided, but there's good money in it. I should probably do something that will bring in some cash."

"Money! I make all the money we need. You should do something interesting. We're getting to be old fogies."

Were we? I studied her as she buttoned her blouse. She looked more beautiful than ever, as many women do after bearing their children. Her long blue-black hair was in a braid, her eyes were dark and deep, and she moved lithely and smoothly, like a jungle cat. She didn't look like a fogie to me.

Maybe I was the fogie. I thought again that perhaps my lifestyle had begun to bore her. After all, how many women would long remain satisfied with a husband who lacked ambition; who had no steady job; who housed his family in an old hunting camp with a leaky porch; who scrounged from the dump and the thrift shop; who straightened used nails; who drove an ancient, rusty Land Cruiser; who loved fishing, loafing with books, drinking beer, cooking, and sipping cold vodka on the rocks; and who aspired to no higher form of life?

The more I thought about it, the more possible it seemed that I was the root of her malaise.

"The job does interest me," I said. "I'm already learning a lot about things I never knew I didn't know."

"There," she said. "I'm presentable, so let's hit the road. It'll be good to see the Skye bunch again!" She ducked past me, paused, came back and gave me a kiss on the cheek, and went on again.

We went in her little Jeep, it being the more civilized of our vehicles, and soon were unloading in front of the Skyes' house. Joshua and Diana immediately spotted a twin with a horse down by the barn and sprinted in that direction. Zee and I were halfway to the house when the front door opened and Mattie came to meet us with hugs and words of welcome. I handed her a bottle of the Jackson house Cabernet Sauvignon (cheap but not bad), and followed the ladies inside.

"The gentlemen are on the back porch with a jug of martinis," said Mattie, leading the way. "We'll join them."

The Skyes' back porch overlooked a lawn rolling down to a small pond, where there were goldfish and frogs and, at the moment, two ducks. The late-afternoon sun cast the shadows of the surrounding oaks across the water, and a small southwest wind hushed through the trees and rippled the surface of the pond.

As we came out through the screened door, John looked up, then put down his drink, climbed out of his chair, and came to meet us.

He shook my hand and exchanged hugs and kisses with Zee. "Zee, let me introduce you to Mahsimba."

Behind him, Mahsimba flowed to his feet. John

turned and Zee and Mahsimba saw each other for the first time. Both hesitated for half a heartbeat, and in that moment I felt some current of energy, some sort of electricity, leap between them as though a switch had been thrown. I saw Zee take a breath and I saw Mahsimba's golden eyes shimmer. Their hands were meeting, lingering, then dropping, and I heard them saying conventional greeting words through smiling lips.

I knew that something very unconventional had just happened even when Mahsimba's hand was shaking mine, even though those liquid eyes looking up into mine were as fathomless as before.

I wondered if John or Mattie had felt what I'd felt. But John was pouring drinks from a crystal pitcher, adding olives (black for Zee, green for me), and passing the martinis to us, giving no sign that anything novel had occurred. And Mattie had seated Zee beside her and the two of them were already catching up on what had happened in their lives during the past months when the Skyes were all up in Weststock and the Jacksons were down here on the Vineyard.

My martini was icy and smooth. It wanted me to drink it fast and have another, but I made myself sip small sips as I found a chair.

"Cheers," said John, lifting his glass. "Well, J.W., have you decided whether you can give Mahsimba some help?"

"I'm interested enough to have spent some time in the library this afternoon catching up on my southern African history and current events in Zimbabwe."

Mahsimba made a small gesture with his hand. "If you have any reservations, please feel free to decline this assignment that your friends have imposed upon you." His eyes flicked toward Zee and then came back. "Your family is certainly more important than my search." He leaned forward and lowered his voice. "And we should remember that at least one man is already dead."

"I think you should take the job." Zee's clear voice surprised me.

"I thought you and Mattie were catching up on last winter," I said.

"We'll finish doing that later." She looked at Mahsimba. "Jeff's told me everything, and he's just the man you need. He was a policeman, he knows the island, and he knows how to snoop."

Snoop. An accurate word, but not one preferred by investigators. J. W. Jackson: snoop.

"And," said Zee, "he's not afraid of much."

Mahsimba's eyes flicked between us.

"I'm afraid of enough things," I said to him. "In this case it isn't a matter of being afraid; it's a matter of me not knowing much. If you know where you want to go and who you want to talk to, I can probably take you there."

"The only name I had when I came here belongs to a dead man," said Mahsimba.

"I don't know how to advise you."

Mahsimba sipped his drink. "I'm told that this island is awash with money. Where there is money, there are places to spend it. I have looked through the Yellow Pages of your telephone book and found listings of many artists and art galleries. I will begin my search by interviewing people in those galleries. The art world is simultaneously vast and small. People know other people, and knowledge and gossip pass rapidly from mouth to ear. Perhaps I will hear a name associated with the eagles. If I do, you can help me find the person. Or perhaps you can make explorations other than mine."

It was like casting for fish in unknown waters. You didn't know if there was anything to catch or, if there was, how to catch it. But as the surf casters say, "If you don't throw, you don't know."

Zee's voice came again: "I think you should do it, Jeff."

I thought of the current that had danced between her and Mahsimba and wondered if my answer had anything to do with that.

"All right," I said. "I'll see what I can do."

"Excellent," said Mahsimba.

Zee cast her eyes around the group and smiled. "To seal the bargain you all have to come to our place for dinner tomorrow. Mahsimba, is there anything you don't eat?"

He smiled. "I am omnivorous, Mrs. Jackson."

Her tongue touched her lips. "Call me Zee," she said. "Just Zee."

7

Since my bluefish wasn't big enough to serve to the crowd that was coming, I stuck the fillets in the freezer and spent the rest of the morning preparing the makings for paella, which, along with French bread and salad, was going to be supper.

Paella is easy to cook, but it takes some time to get the ingredients ready. In this case, I was going to make paella à la Valenciana, using a recipe I'd gotten from a Spanish cookbook written in broken English that I'd found at a yard sale. Long ago some Spanish woman had, according to the introduction, written it for expatriate Englishwomen living in Spain. How it got to Martha's Vineyard was yet another island mystery that I was never going to solve.

When I finished my paella preparations, I used another recipe in the book and made a flan for dessert. My mouth was already watering. Then I got into the truck and drove toward Edgartown to talk with Al Butters about his years in Africa.

As I went, I thought about the previous evening, when Mahsimba, at Zee's urging, had told stories about his experiences in Africa and elsewhere. How he had explored the ruins of Great Zimbabwe; how, when he had worked as a safari guide, he had taken tourists on game walks through the bush, carrying a .458-caliber "walking stick" just in case they ran into some aggressive animal; how a pride of lions could lie down in grass and disappear so completely that you could walk between a dozen cats and never know they were there; how you could usually get an advancing elephant to retreat by stepping forward, holding up your hand, and saying loudly but firmly, "Stop!"; how naive he'd been when he first went to study in Pretoria, and how later he had rowed at Oxford while studying African history.

He was a modest and charming teller of tales, jesting at himself and making light of the perils he had faced and the discoveries he'd made at university. Zee had been enthralled. So had I, for that matter, for he had spoken of places I'd never been and of adventures I'd never imagined. Zee had never seemed more buoyant or bright-eyed as she listened to him and sat beside him at the supper table, talking. Once I'd caught Mattie looking at the two of them. Then she'd glanced at me and met my eyes and looked back at her plate.

We'd left for home with Zee reminding them all that they were coming to our house for supper the next day.

Now the preparations for that supper were complete, and I could begin my efforts to help track down the stone eagles.

My ignorance of the island's art scene was going to be a major disadvantage, but the death of Matthew Duarte was too coincidental with Mahsimba's arrival for me to dismiss the likelihood of a connection between those events. And if, in fact, there was a link between them, a person or persons yet unknown clearly had a powerful interest in the eagles. And where powerful interests are at work, it's always possible that they'll leave some traces of their labor behind.

The questions were just who that person or those persons might be, and why murder, which always attracts the attention of the authorities and is therefore usually a last resort in thoughtful problem solving, had seemed a necessary solution to some dilemma.

Of course it was possible that there really was no hook between Matthew's death and Mahsimba's arrival, and that the cops were probably right to put their money on something much more mundane: a dispute over a woman or money or drugs, or one of the other commonplace causes of killings. For murder's motives are usually as simple and crude as are the weapons and some or all of the actors in the drama. As more than one person has observed, murder victims don't get poisoned in the conservatory by rare venom from some obscure snake native only to the upper Amazon; they get bashed in the head by a brick in an alley. And some drunk, like as not a close friend or relative, did it, not the vicar of Christ Church, who feared that an ancient, forgotten scandal might prevent him from becoming archbishop.

Al and Barbara Butters lived with their dog, Jake, an aging golden retriever, out near Trapps Pond, not far from the beach. If you looked northeast from their wraparound porch you could see Cape Cod on the far side of Nantucket Sound. If you looked northwest you had a good view of the pond. Lately, as money rolled over the island like a tidal wave, huge new houses had been built in the neighborhood, so that the Butters house, which had once seemed large and comfortable, now seemed almost small.

Not so small, however, that claustrophobia made Al and Barbara feel like moving. Their place was plenty big enough for them, Jake, and for their collection of Africana, which they'd bought during the years when they'd lived in Johannesburg, where Al had finished his career in the import-export business.

I hooked left at the Triangle and drove through the parking lot in front of the Your Market liquor store and Trader Fred's emporium, where you can always get good stuff cheap. I took another left on the Oak Bluffs–Edgartown road, then turned right into Cow Bay and took the dirt road to the Butters place. Almost immediately I had to pull over to one side to let Miguel Periera's small, refrigerated truck pass.

Miguel had been a wild island boy, who in his youth was, as they say, "known to the police," and had spent a little time in the gray-bar hotel, but who had then managed to straighten himself out and find his niche in respectable island society. Miguel had done this by creating Periera Food Service, a firm that catered to Vineyarders who rebelled against outrageous island prices and paid him to go off-island and buy them groceries and liquor on the mainland. Periera Food Service now seemed to be doing just fine, thank you.

When both of us had been in our teens, Miguel and I had briefly shared an interest in a girl named Rose Shaw. Rose was another of those young islanders who had not gone off to college after high school but had stayed home instead. Rose, whose prospects were limited at best, had married Jim Abrams, a young neighbor who had almost immediately been drafted and killed in a training exercise, leaving her with his insurance money. She had used it to study art in Boston before returning to the Vineyard and, a few years later, moving in with Miguel without benefit of clergy.

Now Miguel stopped his truck and rolled down his driver's-side window. I did the same. He was a stocky, good-looking guy who looked younger than I knew him to be.

"How ya doin', J.W.?"

"Okay. How's business?"

He gestured at the closest new summer house. "Picking up now the season's coming. Be better as soon as these places start filling up. Not too many people around right now. Season's just getting started."

"You'll be a rich man by Labor Day."

"You can contribute to my retirement plan by giving me an order."

"I'm too poor to be able to afford you, Miguel."

He laughed. "Too cheap, you mean!"

"That, too."

He laughed again and drove on.

The new houses beside the road were gigantic. Like most such houses on the island, they were simply summer "cottages" whose owners presumably had winter mansions somewhere else. There is a lot of money in this world, and a good hunk of it was being spent on Martha's Vineyard, changing the place forever and, many said, for the worse.

The changes that had affected me the most during my island years were not the big new houses but the closing of access to the hunting and fishing spots my father and I and other fishermen and hunters had used when I was a kid. Those locked gates and

NO TRESPASSING signs had begun to appear years before the current money boom.

Frost was right about walls, but the people who had come and were still coming to the island, buying up whatever land was available with their endless money, didn't read Frost, or, if they did, didn't believe him, or, if they believed him, didn't care. I did believe him, so I had no NO TRESPASSING or PRIVATE PROPERTY signs or fences on my fifteen acres.

The Butters house was finished with weathered-gray cedar shingles and circled with a roofed porch. There was a combined garage and barn off to one side and a green lawn tying everything together. Cow Bay had been a quiet place for many years, but was now less so as the new neighboring palaces filled with their summer inhabitants.

I parked and knocked on the door. Barbara Butters opened it.

"Well, J.W. What brings you to these parts? Come in."

Barbara was a sleek sixty-five or so, very neat and slim. She waved me into the front hall as Jake came up wagging his tail to say hello. He sniffed the scents of Oliver Underfoot and Velcro on my hand but let me in anyway. Jake was a proper dog: big and friendly. If you were going to have a dog, Jake was the kind to have.

"There's no wind at all," I said to Barbara, "and I figured that not even Al would go sailing in a dead calm, so I came to see him before it breezes up."

"Smart move. He's in his den, reading about whaling ships in the old days. Go on in."

I did that, passing wall hangings, and shelves holding wood and stone carvings and finely woven baskets, most of which, I knew from past visits, had been brought from southern Africa.

Al Butters's den was a comfortable room, revealing its owner's interests and personality. Its walls were lined with books, more fine African crafts and artwork, and paintings and photos of boats and ships. A chessboard holding a partially played game sat on a small carved table against one wall. Al's desk was in a corner, and an old, worn leather chair sat beneath a reading light. Al climbed out of the chair as I came in and set aside a battered book.

"J.W. Come in."

His hand was leathery but his grip was gentle. He was a hearty-looking seventy or so, weathered by days of sailing. His eyes were sharp and his face was that of a happy man.

"I need some information," I said, "and I thought you might be able to supply it or at least get me pointed in the right direction."

"If I can, I will. What do you need to know?"

"How to find two stone eagles taken from Great Zimbabwe a hundred years ago."

He whistled and his bushy brows lifted. "Is that all?" He waved me toward his desk chair. "It sounds like there's a story here, and I'd like to hear it."

"Me, too," said Barbara, seating herself beside the chess table. "We visited those ruins more than once while we lived in Johannesburg, J.W. They're magnificent."

"I've only seen pictures."

"Someday you'll get there," said Al. "I thought those eagles were all in museums. In fact, we've seen some of them there.

"The floor is yours."

So I told him about the call I'd gotten from Stanley Crandel and about meeting Mahsimba and about the previous day's conversations and events, including the discovery of the body.

"Matthew Duarte, dead?" Barbara put a hand to her lips. "I can't believe it. Why, we saw him at Charles Mauch's party just last week! I must call Connie! Are you sure it was murder?"

"The medical examiner will make the official decision, but I'd say so. Who's Connie?"

"Matthew's wife. She told me at the party that she'd be over on Nantucket this week, visiting friends. She may not even know about what's happened to Matthew. I should tell the police where she is."

She rose and hurried from the room. Al Butters looked into space for a long moment then met my gaze. "Connie's heart may not be broken by the news. The gossip mill has it that Matthew's been talking divorce."

"Another woman?"

He made a small gesture with one hand. "Matthew liked the ladies and they liked him. Connie is his second or third wife."

On Martha's Vineyard it sometimes seems that everyone has been married to everyone else at one time or another. Maybe it's a result of the empty winters, when people have too much time to be bored with their own spouses and to fantasize about their neighbors' husbands and wives.

Al went on. "You say you think there may be a tie-in between Mahsimba's e-mail and Matthew's death?"

I shrugged. "I think it's possible, but it's a police case and they may think differently. Anyway, my situation is that I've agreed to help Mahsimba while he's here on the island, but I don't know where to start. I'm here today because you know African art and you may know other people who share that interest. If the eagles are really on the island, one of those people may know something about them."

He frowned. "I don't think I know any art thieves or murderers, J.W. And I've not heard one word about the two eagles you're looking for."

"I'm not investigating a murder, and I'm not sure the eagles can be considered stolen art. The killing and the eagles may not have anything to do with each other."

"But you think they might."

"I think it's possible," I said. "If there is a link, the police will probably find it anyway. All I'm interested in is locating the birds, but if you want to know the truth, I doubt that they're on the island or ever have been."

"But you still want names."

"Yes. Of people who know about art, especially African art. Maybe one of them knows something or has heard something I can use. Probably not. I've told Mahsimba that I'd nose around."

He rubbed his jaw. "I've heard that murder victims are often killed by people they know. You were a policeman. Is that true?"

"It is as far as I know."

"So Matthew might have been killed by an acquaintance. Someone he knew." He hesitated. "And someone I might know."

I held his gaze. "There was no sign of a break-in at the house."

My impression was that Al's sense of morality was pushing him in ways he didn't want to be pushed, toward a decision he didn't want to make.

He frowned. "Barbara and I know a lot of island people involved in the arts, and most of them knew Matthew Duarte. I can't imagine any of them being criminals, and I'm reluctant to give you their names. I'd feel like an informer. Does that make any sense to you?"

"Of course it does, but I have no reason to think any of your friends is a killer or a thief. I'm just trying to get a line on the two stone eagles."

He shook his head. "No. I'm sorry, J.W., but I just can't do it. You don't remember Joe McCarthy, but I do. If I give you names I'll feel like one of those people who played rat in front of McCarthy. I won't do that to my friends." He pulled a handkerchief from a pocket and wiped his brow.

Joe McCarthy was before my time, but I'd read about him and his investigations.

"All right," I said. "One Joe McCarthy was enough. I don't want to be another one."

"I'm sorry."

"It's all right. Thanks anyway. I'll ask around somewhere else." I stood up.

"I hope you find your eagles, but I'm not sure I want you to find out anything else. I'd hate to see our friends' names spread all over the papers."

"I'm not a cop and I don't work for the newspapers," I said, "so I won't be making any arrests and I won't be publishing any stories. The best scenario I can think of is that somebody will know something about the eagles. The next best is that nobody will know and Mahsimba can go on out to California and hunt his eagles there."

Barbara Butters came into the room. "I've talked to the police. They didn't know where Connie was. They'll try to contact her over on Nantucket."

I thanked them for their time, gave Jake a goodbye pat on the head, and went out into the early-summer sunlight. A light breeze was beginning to stir the leaves on the oak trees around the lawn. I wondered if Al would go sailing today or whether his mind would be on other things. He had looked happy when I'd arrived, but he hadn't looked that way when I left.

I drove home and opened my phone book. Al hadn't supplied me with any names, but Barbara had given me one. I found it: Mauch, first name, Charles.

8

Charles Mauch lived in Vineyard Haven, out toward the lighthouse on West Chop, where there are a lot of large old houses. I knew that some rich and famous people summered in Vineyard Haven, but I had little knowledge of them because their lives and mine were lived in different air. Mauch was one of them.

I made a sandwich for lunch and had a Sam Adams to go with it. Then I phoned the Mauch house. After three rings a woman answered. "Mauch residence."

I gave her my name and told her that I'd like to talk with Mr. Mauch about some artwork.

"J.W. Is that you? This is Rose. Rose Abrams."

Quel surprise. "Rose. It's been a while."

"At least a while. I didn't know you were interested in art."

"And I didn't expect you to answer this phone."

"I work for Charles part-time. I'm sort of a combination assistant and housekeeper. I'm afraid Charles is busy right now. He's working in his study."

"Tell him I was just discussing some artwork with Al and Barbara Butters, and Barbara gave me his name. I won't take up much of his time."

"He doesn't like to be interrupted when he's working, J.W., but since it's you, I'll ask him if he can see you. What is it you want to discuss?"

"Some African stonework. Pretty rare pieces, I'm told."

"Hold on, please." I listened to the silence. Then she came back and said, "Come at two o'clock. He can see you then. He hopes your business won't take too long."

"I hope it won't," I said.

"See you at two, then. How's the family?"

"The kids are both in school now. Joshua is five and Diana is almost four. Time flies."

She didn't seem to notice that I'd said nothing about Zee. Instead, she said, "Yes. Things can change quite a bit, can't they?"

Like the change from Rose Shaw, island kid with little education and no prospects, to Rose Abrams, assistant to Charles Mauch.

I'd read of Mauch in the local papers, usually in regard to artistic events and fund-raisers for worthy causes, and had been told by Barbara Butters that he'd hosted a party attended by the Butterses and Matthew Duarte. It wasn't much knowledge, and I thought I might benefit from having more, so when I drove to Vineyard Haven, I stopped at the library.

The Vineyard Haven library had recently undergone major renovations, including the addition of a controversial columned entrance. I'd thought the new entrance was just fine, but letters to the editors of the island papers had clearly indicated that not everyone agreed with me, the writers' principal criticism apparently being that the columns were just not Vineyardish. The critics had prevailed, the controversial columns had come down, and Martha's

Vineyard had survived yet another assault on its aesthetic traditions.

I got a copy of *Who's Who* from the shelf and sat down at a table.

I was once again not listed, but Charles Mauch was. Yale; philanthropist; board member of major museums, ballet companies, and symphony orchestras; lecturer; author of several books on art; expert on pre-Columbian art in particular; married to Elaine, daughter of a shipping magnate even I had heard of; grown children.

I left the book on the table and drove on out Main Street toward the lighthouse.

Mauch lived on a side street leading down toward the outer harbor. His house was at the end of the lane. It was a big place in the style of the early 1900s, when stucco was in vogue. There were flower gardens around the house and along the front and side fences. A lawn rolled down to the beach, where a boathouse anchored a dock that led out into the harbor. A motor yacht about fifty feet long was tied along one side of the dock and a day sailer, a dinghy, and what looked like a seventeen-foot Boston Whaler were tied to the other side.

There was a circular drive in front of the house, and I parked there, figuring that an old, rusty Land Cruiser with rods on a roof rack would not be too shocking a sight to anyone used to Vineyard vehicles. Even the rich fishermen I knew usually drove their trucks until they rusted out, as a matter of pride and frugality. Mine, of course, was driven out of necessity, since I couldn't afford anything better.

I knocked on the door and Rose Abrams opened it. She had a smile on her face and was wearing comfortable, informal clothes. They were well tailored, but something about the lines and material told even me that they weren't too expensive, so I figured that although Rose was functioning on a higher social plane than when we'd dated long ago, she still didn't really have the big bucks. On Martha's Vineyard, rich people often wear sloppy, old, ratty clothes, but they are clothes that had once cost a lot. You can spot a rich girl a block away.

"J.W. Come in, please. Charles is in his study."

Charles. Not Mr. Mauch. "You're looking good," I said, meaning it. "I ran into Miguel this morning. Old home week."

Her lips formed a smile. "It's a small island. Follow me, please."

We went down a corridor hung with paintings and into a room lined with books and decorated with small, exquisite *objets d'art*. There was a couch against the far wall, under a window overlooking the harbor. A tall, lean, white-haired man stood up from an ornate desk as we came through the door. The desk was covered with books and papers surrounding a computer. I must have been the only man in America without a desk with a computer on it.

"Mr. Jackson is here," said Rose.

"Thank you, Rose."

She inclined her head and went back past me into the hall, closing the door behind her.

"I'm Charles Mauch," he said, putting out his hand, which I took. He smiled a warm, personal smile, and I thought he was probably a very successful winner of confidences and extractor of donations for the artistic organizations to which he belonged.

"J. W. Jackson."

"How may I be of assistance? Rose said you mentioned works of art. Please, sit down."

I sat in a leather chair with a high back topped by a gilded crest. "I won't be long. I see that you're busy."

He smiled again and made a small, graceful gesture that indicated he was indeed busy but he was more than pleased to give me all of his attention for as long as I needed it.

"Someone once observed that the graveyards are full of indispensable men, Mr. Jackson. Similarly, if my indispensable paper never gets written, the sun will rise anyway. Tell me how I can help you."

"I've been asked by a friend to try to locate two art objects from Africa. I went to see Al and Barbara Butters. They couldn't help, but your name came up, so here I am."

"African art is not my specialty, Mr. Jackson. What is it in particular that you're looking for?"

"Two soapstone carvings from Zimbabwe. Birds."

He studied me for a long moment, then said, "That's rather vague. Can you be more precise?"

"I've never seen them. I know they're old. They're carved eagles that were originally found during the early excavations of what's now known as Great Zimbabwe and became part of a private collection. Just before the Ian Smith government of Rhodesia lost power, the birds apparently disappeared from the private collection. The Zimbabwean government has been trying to find them for years. There's evidence that a former mercenary brought them to America and that they possibly ended up on the Vineyard."

"Indeed?"

I told him about Brownington's efforts in California and Mahsimba's belief that Matthew Duarte might have handled the sale. "I got involved because I know the island fairly well," I said, "and because a friend asked me to help out."

He nodded. "May I ask who that friend might be?"

"His name is Stanley Crandel. He summers in Oak Bluffs and got interested in the eagles as the result of a trip to Africa, where he met Mahsimba. I'm working for Mahsimba."

"I believe I've met Mr. Crandel." Mauch's expression was thoughtful. "Is the United States government involved in this matter?"

"Not that I know of. Why?"

"Because a great deal of stolen art is being transported over international borders. It's a thriving trade involving millions of dollars, and various nations, including ours, are interested in stopping it."

"I've read about it. I'm not sure who legally owns these eagles. They were taken from Africa thirty-five or so years ago, and before that their ownership was debatable."

His voice became professorial. "There's an art-loss registry that has lists and pictures of items stolen or missing, but I don't remember ever seeing a reference to your eagles. Aside from stolen art, there's the issue of museums having acquired materials from other countries that now want them back. Greece's battle with Britain for the return of the Elgin marbles is probably the best-known example of that."

"I've read about that."

"It's a contentious matter because the museums often purchased the materials long ago or at least were not discouraged from taking them from their native lands. It's also arguable that had they not taken them and preserved them, the materials would have long since been destroyed. Did you know, for example, that before the British government began protecting Stonehenge, tourists were given hammers and chisels and encouraged to chop off souvenirs from the stones, or that locals used the monument as a stone quarry for building materials for their houses and barns?"

"I remember reading something about it."

"You apparently read a great deal, Mr. Jackson. Are you involved in archaeology or the arts yourself?"

"No. I'm a fisherman. That's why I need your help. You're well-known in your field and you know others in it. I'm trying to find out if you or anyone you know might have seen or heard about these Zimbabwe eagles."

The phone on his desk rang, but he ignored it. "Rose will get that," he said. "She takes my calls and filters the ones I need to answer. Well, you've taken a logical first step in coming to me. I know of the eagles in the African museums, of course, but I'm afraid I personally have heard nothing of the ones you seek. Al Butters probably knows other islanders with an interest in African art, but you've already talked with him and Barbara."

He frowned and was silent for a moment. "Perhaps your best bet would be to talk with Matt Duarte. His father, Dan, who you say was interviewed by that fellow Brownington, was a notable art dealer. Dan and I went way back, all the way to Yale. He died just last December, as you may know. Auto accident. A tragic loss. Matt lives in West Tisbury. The East Coast rep for the firm, as it were. I'd go see him, if I were you."

There was a rap on the door and Rose Abrams came in just as I said, "I'm afraid Matthew Duarte won't be telling me anything. He's dead." I glanced at Rose, saw the color fade from her face, then looked quickly back at Mauch. His eyes were wide. I hesitated, then added, "Apparently it was murder. He was shot in the head."

Behind me, Rose gave a small cry. I turned, then leaped up and ran to her just in time to keep her from slipping to the floor. I half carried her to my chair and eased her down into it.

"I'm afraid I've given her a shock," I said. "Where's your kitchen? I'll get some water."

"Down the hall to the left." Mauch began to massage her hands. He looked at me. "She's not the only one who's shocked! Hurry with that water."

I went down the hall into a large, modern kitchen, found a glass and filled it from the faucet, and came back to the study, where I heard Rose Abrams say, "I'm all right, Charles, really."

I handed the glass to him and he put it to her lips.

"Thank you," she said. "I'll be fine. It's just that . . ."

Mauch looked angrily at me. "You might have been discreet, man! Did you have to blurt it out like that? Before a woman?"

His, apparently, was an old-fashioned chivalry, wherein women were perceived as delicate creatures who needed to be sheltered from the hard realities of the world.

"Sorry," I said to Rose. "I should have stopped talking when you came in."

She reached down into herself and found strength and will enough to straighten herself in her chair. "It's not your fault, J.W., I . . ." She paused, then looked at Mauch. "I almost forgot. Mr. Harper from the Smithsonian is on the phone. You wanted me to put him through if he called. Oh, dear, how long has he been on hold?"

"Never mind that, Rose. Harper can wait a few minutes. How are you feeling?"

She sipped more water and took the glass in her hands. "Much better. Please talk with Mr. Harper. I'll be fine."

"You sit there, then," said Mauch. "I'll take the call in the bedroom. Stay with her if you will, Jackson. I'll be right back."

He strode from the room. I looked down at Rose and thought that she wasn't as all right as she'd said. Her face was snow-white and the water glass was trembling in her hand.

"I'm sorry I shocked you," I said. "I take it that you knew Matthew Duarte quite well."

"I worked for Matt when I wasn't working here." She looked at me with stunned eyes. "He was murdered?"

"It looks that way."

"Shot?"

"Yes. In his own living room."

I caught her as she slumped forward and carried her to the couch. The glass had fallen from her hand.

9

At home I thought about things while I set the supper table and got the house straightened for the evening's guests. Then I called Al Butters's number and had a stroke of luck, because Barbara answered. She'd been out of the room when Al had declined to give me any names, and there was a chance he hadn't told her about his refusal.

After we'd exchanged hellos, I said, "I've just finished having a talk with Charles Mauch up in Vineyard Haven. While I was there I told him about Matthew Duarte's death. Mauch's assistant, Rose Abrams, was there. She fainted when she heard the news. Do you know her?"

"That bitch!" said Barbara in a voice like a snake's hiss.

I immediately thought I knew the answer to my next question, but I asked it anyway: "Why would Rose Abrams have had such a strong reaction?"

"Because she's been breaking up Connie's marriage! During the past year that witch Rose Abrams has been sleeping with Matthew Duarte more than Connie has."

"I heard he liked the ladies. What was his appeal? What was hers?"

"You know the cliché: Men can't resist beauty; women can't resist money. She's young and pretty, and he was rich. She got into his bed and wanted into his bank account. Tough luck for her that he got himself killed before the divorce went through, the slut. Men!"

"She didn't seem quite that tough when she heard he was dead."

Barbara snorted. "She fainted at the loss of his bank account."

I had to laugh. "You're a mean one, Mr. Grinch. Connie is your friend, I take it. You've been on her side."

"She's my friend, and now she doesn't have to worry about Matt and his money going to that trollop."

I said the obvious. "The cops might think that's a motive for murder."

"They'd be wrong. Connie was on Nantucket when it happened and she's not the type who'd know where to find a killer for hire. Besides, knowing her, she'd rather have Matt alive, even if he took his money with him when he left her. She's too sweet for her own good."

"Is there a lot of money involved?"

"He had his share, I guess. There's a flood of money on the island right now, as I'm sure you know, and the people who have it aren't afraid to spend it on art, to say nothing of houses or yachts or whatever else their little hearts desire. I know that Matt had a special room in his barn just for storing merchandise until he sold it. It's air-conditioned or temperature-controlled, or whatever they do in rooms like that. He worked with his father, you know, and Daniel Duarte had a worldwide reputation."

"So I'm told. There's a possibility that Matthew

knew about those Zimbabwe eagles I mentioned when I was at your place this morning. Since he's dead, I can't talk with him about them. Can you help me out? Do you know anyone else I can talk to? Anyone with an interest in African art?"

She was silent for a moment, then said, "There are a couple of folks who have collections that make ours look tiny. Georgie Hall is one of them. Do you know Georgie and Brent?"

"No, I don't."

"She's the collector, but Brent pays the freight. He can afford it. Another person is Gerald Jenkins. His collection is smaller than Georgie's but he has a better eye than she does. Rumor has it that Georgie envies his taste and tries to compensate by buying more expensive things than Gerry can afford. Am I being catty?"

"I don't mind. I'm a cat man."

"All right, then, I'll give you another rumor: Georgie sometimes gets a line on something Gerry wants and buys it first for more money than Gerry can offer."

"How does she manage that?"

"The art business is no different than any other business. Dealers are interested in making money. They aren't above arranging bidding wars among clients. Matt did a bit of that himself, I'd say."

"They must have to walk a thin line, for fear of offending good customers."

She laughed. "Maybe they do when things are tight, but there's so much money around these days that they don't have to worry about losing a customer or two."

"Not even a Gerald Jenkins?"

"Not even Gerry."

"Where can I find Mr. Jenkins and Mrs. Hall?"

"Try the telephone book. If you can't find them there, come down here and I'll draw you a map."

I rang off and opened my telephone book. Sure enough, there they were, listed just like ordinary folks. Was this a wonderful country, or what?

Gerald Jenkins lived off Middle Road, and Brent Hall lived on Tea Lane. They were almost neighbors and both also lived not far from the house and barn once owned by the late Matthew Duarte. I wondered if there was any significance to that, but set the question aside because a lot of people lived in Chilmark, and understandably so, since it's the loveliest township on the island. If I didn't live where I live, and if I had a dozen buckets of large-denomination bills to spend on a house, and if it weren't so far from the nearest liquor store, I'd live in Chilmark myself.

A glance at my watch suggested that I didn't have time to make a trip up-island and back before the kids got home and supper guests arrived, so I contented myself with a Sam Adams while I double-checked my paella makings and table setting. I hadn't finished the beer when I heard a car coming down our long, sandy driveway. I went to the front porch in time to see Zee's little Jeep come into the yard.

Zee parked and got out. She was carrying a paper bag sporting a name I remembered seeing on a window in Vineyard Haven.

"You're early," I said.

She gave me a fast kiss. "I want to take a shower and change before the kids get home." She smiled and went into the house.

She was in our bedroom, humming to herself while she brushed her hair, when the kids came running down the road from where the bus had dropped them off. One sign of youth is the unnecessary expenditure of energy. The older I get, the more I'm inclined to the "never stand if you can sit, never sit if you can lie down" school of exercise.

"Hi, Pa."

"Hi, Josh and Diana. How was school?"

"It was okay."

"What did you do?"

"Nothing much." Joshua glanced at the Jeep. "Is Ma home already?"

"Yes, she is."

"Oh, good!" Diana ran into the house.

"She's early," said Joshua.

"She wanted to take a shower. We're having company for supper. The Skyes and their guest, Mahsimba."

"What are we going to eat?"

"Paella."

He looked pleased. "I love paella. So does Diana."

Diana the huntress was always on the trail of food. She would eat anything. "You look like you could stand a shower, too," I said.

"I'll use the outdoor one," he said, and disappeared.

Clearly a lad with healthy instincts. An outdoor shower is infinitely superior to an indoor one; you never have to worry about cleaning it afterward, you can see the sky, and it never gets stuffy. We used ours for eight or nine months of the year, abandoning it only in midwinter, when the pipes might freeze. Show me a person who doesn't like an outdoor shower, and I'll show you someone who probably likes small dogs—someone whose company you should avoid.

About ten minutes before our guests were scheduled to arrive, Zee emerged from the bedroom looking sleek and bright as a tiger in the forests of the night. Her hair fell over her shoulders like dark fire, and her eyes were deep as oceans. I hadn't seen that dress before.

I eyed her appreciatively, and she gave me an odd, almost nervous smile.

"How about a drink?" I said. "You look terrific, by the way."

"Thank you. Yes, I'd like a drink."

I got the Luksosowa and two chilled glasses out of the freezer, swirled dry vermouth in the glasses, and then tossed it out and filled the glasses with the vodka. Two black olives in Zee's, two green ones stuffed with peppers in mine. Perfect martinis.

She sipped her drink. She had the look of one of those girl-women you sometimes see on college campuses who radiate sexuality but who still aren't quite grown-up.

"Let's go up on the balcony," I said.

"Sure." She led the way.

There was a northeast wind ruffling the water, and I could clearly see Cape Cod looming across Nantucket Sound. The trees were gently moving. I looked at Zee and she smiled that odd smile again.

I heard a car coming down the driveway. Zee stood and looked in that direction. John Skye's Jeep came into view.

"There they are," I said, and went down the stairs.

I heard Zee start after me, pause, then continue down again. Joshua and Diana came scampering.

John, Mattie, the twins, and Mahsimba got out of the car. I kissed Mattie, Zee kissed both Mattie and John, and the twins were hugged by our children, who immediately invited them to the tree house. Not everyone got invited to the tree house, and Jill and Jen were aware of the honor being bestowed upon them, so they went, laughing.

I shook hands with John and with Mahsimba. Mahsimba shook hands with Zee. "It's very kind of you to invite us," he said to her.

"We're glad you could come," she said. Their hands lingered, then parted.

"Let's get you all some drinks and then we'll go up onto the balcony," I said.

Mahsimba was looking at the gardens. "You have a lovely place, Mrs. Jackson."

She never took her eyes from his face. "Call me Zee. Would you like a tour of the estate?"

He smiled a quick, white-toothed smile. "Very much."

Zee led him away while I waved the others into the house. At the door I glanced back. She had taken his arm as they walked between the flower beds.

10

At the supper table I caught Mattie looking at Zee, who was seated between Mahsimba and John and listening to Mahsimba. Mattie flicked her eyes at me before looking back at her plate.

Mahsimba had been speaking of his onetime job as a safari guide and describing the difference between hyena and cheetah spoor. "Not," he concluded, "that you will really need that knowledge here on your beautiful island!"

Zee and John laughed.

"Tell us about the murder, J.W.," said a twin. "Daddy and Mahsimba won't tell us anything. You'd think we were little kids instead of college students."

"Yeah, Pa," chimed in Joshua. "Tell us about the murder!"

"You *are* just a kid," said the twin, "so you shouldn't listen." She fluttered her eyelashes at me. "But you can tell us big people, J.W. Please! We're going to read about it in the papers anyway, you know, so why not just tell us?"

I looked at John. He shrugged. So I gave a factual description of what we'd seen, leaving out speculation.

"You mean you can't even be sure it was murder?" asked a twin, disappointed by the starkness of my report.

"He was dead, but the authorities will have to decide if it was murder."

"What do you think?"

"I'm told he was shot in the head, and I didn't see any gun lying around."

"Murder for sure," said the twin, cheering up.

"Who did it?" asked her sister.

"The police are trying to find out."

"Whoever it was, the victim let him in, isn't that right?"

"I didn't see any sign of a forced entry."

"It was somebody he knew, then."

"Maybe."

"Let's change the subject," suggested Mattie. She turned to Mahsimba. "How's the search for the eagles going?"

He sipped his wine. "Slowly. There are a remarkable number of galleries and studios on your little island, and I have only begun to visit them. I have many more people to talk to."

"Have you learned anything useful?"

He shrugged. "You don't always know at the time you get it whether information is useful. It's dull work, I'm afraid. So far, I've learned little that seems important." He looked at me. "And you, J.W., have you made any progress?"

I told them about my day. Mahsimba listened carefully, and said not a word.

But a twin was not so silent. "The woman fainted, you say! Ah-ha!" She and her sister exchanged wide-eyed, knowing nods.

I wished I could tell them apart, but I couldn't. "Ah-ha, what?" I asked. "Some women faint all the time."

"Pooh," said a twin. "Women hardly ever faint anymore. Ever since they gave up corsets they've been fine. No, she fainted because she was shocked, really shocked. And you know what that means?"

"It means he was her lover!" cried her sister. "Yes!"

"Her heart has been broken!"

"Now, girls, don't be melodramatic," cautioned their mother.

"And we know another thing, too," said a twin, raising a finger.

"What's that?" I asked.

"We know she didn't do it. She didn't kill him. If she'd killed him, she wouldn't have been shocked at the news." The twins looked at each other and simultaneously exclaimed, "We should be detectives!"

"Defectives are what you are," said John.

"All right, girls," said Mattie, "clear the table and let J.W. and Mahsimba talk. And wash the dishes while you're at it!"

"I'll take care of the dishes later," I said. "Right now it's time for Joshua and Diana to be in bed."

"Aw, Pa, it's early."

"You were up late last night and you have school tomorrow."

"Aw, Pa."

But they said their good-nights and went to their rooms while the twins cleared.

"We'll be glad to do the dishes, J.W.," said a twin, and soon there was only coffee and cognac on the table.

"I've heard of this man Mauch," said Mahsimba. "He is very well known. I wonder if he is a descendant of the German, Carl Mauch, who visited the ruins of Great Zimbabwe in 1871."

"I didn't ask him, though maybe I should have."

"The other people you've named, Jenkins and Hall, are not familiar to me. Tomorrow, I'll ask about them as I continue my visits. Perhaps I'll learn something I might otherwise have missed."

"And I'll talk with them in person, if I can." I looked at him. "One thing Mauch said that interested me was that Daniel Duarte was killed last December in an auto accident. I don't remember you mentioning that."

Mahsimba studied me, then seemed to come to some decision. "I hope I've not offended you." He seemed confident that he hadn't, and his confidence was justified.

"My feelings aren't hurt," I said. "People usually only tell you what they want you to hear."

He nodded. "Quite so. When first we spoke, I wasn't sure that Daniel Duarte's death was relevant to the work you were considering undertaking. That was, of course, before you told me of your Headless Horseman and before we discovered Matthew Duarte's body."

"But now things are different."

"Yes. Now, if I was to speculate on the significance of the death of Daniel Duarte, I would point out that only days after David Brownington saw him, Duarte died in an automobile accident and I would note that one of Brownington's skills was in arranging such accidents."

If that was one of Brownington's skills, and Brownington and Mahsimba shared a past, I wondered if Mahsimba had the same skill.

"Why would he kill Daniel Duarte?" I asked.

"Perhaps to send a message to others who might otherwise be reluctant to talk."

"To Matthew Duarte, for instance?"

"Exactly."

"What about Parsons, the mercenary? Did Brownington kill him, too?"

Mahsimba shook his head. "No practical person commits violence unless there is a good reason for it. Once Brownington knew about Matthew Duarte, there was no longer any reason to be concerned about Parsons. Parsons spent the money he got for the birds and is a sick old man who probably doesn't have long to live, anyway. God will be allowed to take Parsons in his own time."

"God got some help with both Duartes. And if Brownington is dead, who killed him? And who killed Matthew Duarte? Someone who didn't want him talking to you?"

Mahsimba sipped his coffee. "People involved in illegal activities have a greater chance of being murdered than people who aren't."

"Do you think Matthew revealed the name of the buyer of the eagles before he was shot?"

"If he had done that, there would have been no need to kill him."

It was my turn to nod. "And if he refused to tell, his interrogators would have been fools to kill him, since he was the only person who knew the name of the buyer. Maybe they killed Brownington, though, to keep him from persuading Matthew to talk."

Mahsimba's face revealed nothing of his thoughts.

I went on. "The police will be investigating, and they're more likely than we are to find out who killed who, and why. Of course, the Horseman may not be Brownington and Duarte may not have been killed because of the eagles. I'd guess that the first person they'll be talking to is Connie Duarte. And the second one will be Rose Abrams."

"*Cherchez la femme*. Yes."

"Two male chauvinists!" Zee feigned anger then laughed as Mahsimba looked at her first with surprise, then with a smile. She touched his arm. "I'm joking!"

"In any event," he said, "while I wait for whatever information the police may discover, tomorrow I plan to continue my visits to the island's galleries."

"And I'll try to talk with Gerald Jenkins and Georgie Hall," I said.

Later, after we said our good-nights, I went into the house, but Zee stood in the yard and watched John's Jeep disappear up the driveway. When she came inside, her dark eyes seemed full of dreams.

11

I waited until a reasonable hour the next morning, then phoned Gerald Jenkins. When he answered, I said, "My name is Jackson. I got your name from Barbara Butters. I'm working for a man who has an interest in two particular examples of African art. I'm hoping that you can give me some information about them."

He sounded annoyed. "I'm not in the consulting business, Mr. Jackson."

"I'm not a buyer or a seller. In fact, I know almost nothing about African art or any other kind. That's why I'd like to talk with you. I won't take up much of your time."

"What are these pieces? Do you have them with you?"

"They're carvings. I don't have them with me, but I can show you a photograph."

"Photos don't always show much."

"I'll be glad to hear anything you have to say when you see them. I think they might interest you. They're old pieces."

I listened to some silence, then he said, "All right, you've tempted me. Can you be here in an hour?"

"Yes. Thanks."

I had time to do a bit of work in the yard before heading up-island. While I extracted some weeds from the raised vegetable gardens, I thought about things said and unsaid of late. I felt almost removed from my own body, as though I were watching myself from a short distance away. I knew what I was feeling and thinking, but it was as though I were only an observer of those experiences.

And as I observed myself from outside, it occurred to me that Zee might also be feeling that way because she had killed a man. She knew that she had done the necessary thing, the right thing, but knowing and feeling are not the same. And now, perhaps, Zee was outside of herself, watching her life but not really being a part of it, as though it were a play and she were an actress.

When I remembered to look at my watch, I realized that I had left myself no traveling time to spare. I drove to Chilmark, where, leading off Middle Road, one of the island's most beautiful lanes, I came to Gerald Jenkins's driveway.

His name was on his mailbox, and his driveway was a narrow one, winding up toward Prospect Hill until it opened into a small meadow containing a house that, like that of Al and Barbara Butters, once might have been considered large, but was now modest compared with the places being built by the new money that was drowning the island.

There were outbuildings to one side and a looping driveway in front. The house itself had a fine view of Menemsha Pond and points west, north, and south. No Man's Land and the Elizabeth Islands were visible in the hazy distance.

I parked and knocked on the front door. The man who opened it wore a white summer shirt and slacks. He appeared to be about sixty years old,

although it's hard for me to guess how old people are
these days. Some twelve-year-old girls look as old as
their mothers, and some of their mothers could be
sixteen. I knew I could no longer trust my judgment
about age when cops and doctors began to resemble
high school students.

"I'm J. W. Jackson," I said.

"Come in."

He held the door and I walked into what appeared
to be a private museum. African art was displayed
everywhere, in the form of stone, wood, metal, tex-
tiles. Even I could see that it was very fine.

Jenkins noted my interest. He gestured as we
walked: "A Masai shield. Cowhide with a wooden rim.
The painted patterns show the owner's clan. Early
nineteenth century."

"Lion killers, I've been told."

"Yes. They used spears. Protectors of their own
cattle herds and raiders of other herds. This is an
Ashanti chief's helmet. From Ghana. The orna-
ments are gold. This is a Sande mask from Sierra
Leone. This bronze is from Benin. Sixteenth century.
A favorite of mine. So is this head, which is even ear-
lier. It's from Ife. Lost wax technique. Common in
West Africa."

"I'm impressed."

"Thank you. Here's my office. Sit down there.
Now, what can I do for you?"

The office, too, was adorned with art objects taste-
fully arranged. "Aren't you worried about thieves?"
I asked.

He cocked his head to one side. "Why do you
ask? Are you a thief, Mr. Jackson?"

"Not yet, but if I had enough room in my house

to display this stuff, I might consider becoming one."

He studied me, then smiled. "If you don't have room for it in your house, you could sell it for a good deal of money. There are people right here on the Vineyard who would pay a pretty penny for what's here."

"Are there? I didn't notice any security system."

"Oh? Do you know about security systems, Mr. Jackson?"

"Not much. Still, valuable collections of art aren't usually left in unguarded houses. One man I know of kept his in a special, air-conditioned room under lock and key. You don't. I'm a little surprised, is all."

"Do you lock away your favorite things, Mr. Jackson?"

"I have nothing of great value except my wife and children. I don't lock them away, of course."

"Some men do, I'm told."

"Yes. They think their families are their possessions."

"You disagree."

I thought of Zee. "I don't believe in slavery. I love my family and I'll protect them, but I don't own them. My fishing gear is probably the most valuable stuff I actually own, and it's right out there in plain sight."

He nodded. "I've been advised to put my things in a safer place, but I want to see them. I want them around me. I want to be able to touch them. So I keep them here with me, not in some vault. I have strong locks on my doors and bars on my windows and, although you can't see it, an alarm system linked to our police station. If anyone breaks in, the alarm is supposed to go off, or I can trip it myself if I'm here when the thieves arrive. I've never been sure that it works."

"Your insurance premiums must be dandies."

"I can't afford to insure my things. I have more money than some people, but not so much as many others. I have to be careful about how I spend it. I prefer to buy rather than to insure."

I looked at him with new interest. "I know fishermen with the same problem. They have to sail uninsured boats. They risk everything every time they go out, but they have no choice. You're very open about your security, such as it is. A lot of people try to keep such information secret."

"I prefer openness. I want people to know about my locks and alarm. I'm telling you, a perfect stranger, for instance. I also make no secret about the items in my collection. The better known they are, the less likely they are to be successfully resold if stolen. My lawyer has written descriptions and photos of everything I own, so if something ever is pilfered, its image can be immediately made known to all potential buyers. Most of them are honest, though, of course, a few are not." He paused. "I also have a pistol that I know how to use."

Another surprise. "And would you use it on a thief?"

"Without hesitation."

"What caliber?"

"Forty-five."

I felt a smile on my face. "Forty-five more reasons for me to give up the idea of art theft as a career." I took the photo of the eagles from my pocket and handed it to him. "Here, these are the objects I'm interested in. What can you tell me about them?"

He studied the fuzzy photo under a desk light. "They appear to be soapstone eagles such as were found in the ruins of Great Zimbabwe. They resemble the chevron eagle, but my recollection of that bird is that the beak is missing. These two have beaks, and there are crocodiles on the pedestals." He handed the photo back to me. "I really can't tell much more than that from this photo. Where was it taken, and when?"

"I'm told it was taken in Rhodesia sometime before it became Zimbabwe. Are the birds real or fakes?"

"It's impossible to say. I'd have to see them. You told me you were working for a man with an interest in the birds. Does he have them? If they're available, I'd love to examine them."

"He's looking for them. I'm trying to help him."

"Here on Martha's Vineyard?" His eyes grew bright.

"It's possible that they're here or were at one time. You must know most of the island's collectors and dealers. Have you heard anyone say anything about such birds?"

He sat back and studied me, then shook his head. "I've heard nothing. Tell me why you think the birds might be here."

"Matthew Duarte's father's firm sold them. Matthew may have been the agent for the sale."

"Matthew Duarte?" He gave a little nod. "Ah."

It was my turn to cock my head. *"Ah?"*

He touched his fingers together. "Clearly you should talk with Matthew."

"I'd need a medium to do that. Matthew Duarte was shot to death the day before yesterday. I imagined that you'd heard."

He looked surprised but not shocked. "I haven't been listening to the news. How did it happen?"

"The police are investigating. The gun wasn't on the scene, so it looks like homicide."

He became thoughtful. "Matthew Duarte shot, eh? Well, well."

"You don't seem too disturbed."

He looked around the room. "No. No, I'm not disturbed. I mean, it's probably always a surprise when someone you know is murdered." He brought his eyes back to mine. "But it's less of a surprise when it happens to some people rather than to others."

"What do you mean?"

"I mean that Matthew Duarte was thought by some people to be a dealer in stolen goods, and that thieves fall out with one another, sometimes violently."

"What makes you think Duarte was a criminal?"

He shrugged. "I have no personal evidence that he was, but that is the gossip." Then his tone changed. "I do know that the man was short on ethics."

"How so?"

His voice became bitter. "I located a fine Bakuba sculpture. A portrait statue of a king, probably seventeenth century. I arranged the purchase through Matthew Duarte, but once it was in his hands, Duarte was offered more money than we had agreed to, and he sold it to the higher bidder. We had no formal contract, so there was nothing I could do. I've conducted no business with him since, and I'm inclined to believe the rumors about him. I would not wish him dead, but I'll not mourn him, either."

"Had Duarte double-crossed anyone else?"

"I suspect that mine was not an isolated case."

"So he had enemies."

He shrugged. "If so, he deserved them."

"Can you suggest anyone else who might be of help to me in finding the eagles?"

"Charles Mauch is the sort of man who might be able to help you. He knows everyone and has long ears."

"I've talked with him and he said he'd heard nothing."

He frowned, then said, "You might talk with Georgie Hall. She lives not far from here, over on Tea Lane. Unlike me, she has an unlimited amount of money, and I know she and Matthew Duarte had business dealings."

"If you think of anyone else, will you let me know?"

"Very well. I'd like to see the birds myself."

"If I find them, I'll try to arrange a showing." Then, because I rather liked him, I said, "I think you should expect a call from the police. Unless they find Duarte's killer quickly, they'll want to interview his acquaintances."

He smiled grimly. "Especially those who own pistols and who had reason to dislike him?"

12

Tea Lane supposedly got its name from the pre-Revolutionary activities of Captain Robert Hillman, who avoided paying the taxes on his tea by smuggling it to the Vineyard and hiding it so well that the authorities could never find it. Good for Captain Robert, I say.

I once was reading a novel wherein the protagonist, who was driving down Tea Lane, had a revelation of some sort, threw a U-turn, and drove back the other way. Since Tea Lane is so narrow that such a turn is impossible, I stopped reading the book. Literary snobbery takes many forms.

Since Zee keeps our cell phone in her car, I drove to Menemsha and used a public phone to call Georgie Hall. When she answered, I gave her the same story I'd given Gerald Jenkins.

"You say that Barbara Butters gave you my name? What did she tell you about me?" Georgie's tone seemed defensive, as though she was doubtful that Barbara Butters would have said anything nice about her.

"She told me that you had a large collection of art and that you might be able to tell me something about the pieces that interest the man I'm working with."

"And who might that man be?"

It was a question Gerald Jenkins hadn't asked. "His name is Abraham Mahsimba. Do you know him?"

"Sounds like a foreigner."

"He's from Africa. He's a friend of Stanley Crandel."

"I don't know him either."

"Crandel Supermarkets, Crandel Publications, Crandel this and that. Perhaps your husband knows of him. Stanley phoned me from London and asked me to lend Mahsimba a hand. I'd appreciate any help you can give me." Since flattery gets you far with most people, I tried a small lie. "I'm told you're an expert on art."

She gave a modest little laugh. "Well, I don't know that I'd go that far, but . . . I have a luncheon date at one. Can you be here in half an hour?"

"I'm in Menemsha. I can be there in ten minutes."

She gave me directions.

Mr. and Mrs. Brent Hall lived at the end of a new, paved driveway in a trophy house that looked toward Vineyard Sound and the Elizabeth Islands. Through the light haze I could see the mainland on the far side of Buzzards Bay. The house looked like the best that money could buy, and if I had more sensitivity I might have been embarrassed to park my rusty Land Cruiser in front of the stone steps leading up to the wide porch; but I didn't.

The woman who answered my knock was soft, middle-aged, and dressed in pastel clothes such as wealthy women buy for lunches and cocktail parties. Her hair was yellow and her handshake was fleeting. I followed her into a huge entrance hall.

The house struck me as looking like a series of photos in *House Beautiful* or a coffee-table book on elegant summer living. There was no sign that real people lived in it; everything was perfect and untouched; no wrinkles in the rugs, no indication that anything had ever been used. Even the magazines on a side table had been arranged for effect.

I pretended to be awed. "This is really lovely."

"We like it. It's very Vineyard, we think."

She lived on a different Vineyard than I did.

In a niche in the far wall sat a piece of art that I suspected I recognized. "That's an impressive object," I said.

"Yes, it is interesting, isn't it? One of my newest purchases. A portrait sculpture of a Bakuba king. Probably from the sixteen hundreds. Are you interested in African art, Mr. Jackson?"

"I don't know much about it, but I'm glad to know that you do, since the pieces I'm interested in are African. Personally, I lean more toward Russell and Remington." I smiled the nervous smile of a peasant in the presence of a queen.

Seeing it, the queen was gracious. "My dear husband, bless his soul, would understand you perfectly. He's simply in love with the American frontier period but knows nothing at all about what artifacts are good and what are bad. I have to do all his buying for him. Let me show you his den. You men are all the same, ha! ha! You'll love it!"

She led me to what looked like a Victorian gentlemen's club room. There were animal heads and a small arsenal of weapons on the walls, and animal skins on the floor. The chairs were of ancient leather, and there was a bar on the far side of the room beside a bookcase filled about fifty-fifty with leather-bound tomes and more modern books about the American West.

Georgie Hall made a sweeping gesture with one arm. "Brent just adores this room, but I've had to buy everything in it because the dear man has no taste at all!"

"It's very impressive."

"Isn't it? Those weapons, for example, were all once owned by well-known men of the frontier. I know nothing about such things myself, naturally, but I buy only historic firearms with authentic histories." She pointed with a bejeweled hand. "My husband is particularly fond of that one, because it once belonged to Jesse James and dear Brent is a great Jesse James fan! I got it from poor, dear Matthew Duarte just last January, for Brent's birthday. He was ever so pleased!"

"I'm sure he was." I read a gilt-rimmed card that identified the weapon as a forty-one-caliber double-action Colt, model 1889, and informed me that it had indeed once belonged to the famous outlaw.

"And this Winchester rifle was once owned by Buffalo Bill! It cost me a pretty penny, but the look on Brent's face when I gave it to him made it worth every cent!"

"I can imagine."

The card describing the rifle as a "One in One Thousand" and authenticating its previous ownership by William F. Cody was rimmed in gold, as were the cards beneath every weapon on the wall. The cards gave Brent Hall's den something of the feeling of a museum.

"Now, I know you'd love to stay right here in this room," said Mrs. Hall, giving a little laugh, "but we must get down to business, I'm afraid." She led me back into the room we'd been in before, where she sat in an overstuffed chair and pointed me to another one. "How can I help you, Mr. Jackson?"

I handed her the photo of the eagles. "I'm looking for these birds. I'm hoping that you've seen them or heard of them."

She stared myopically at the photo, then held it up to the light. "Oh, dear. I'm afraid I need my spectacles. Would you be kind enough to fetch them for me? I believe they're over on that reading table."

I pronounced my delight to be of service and went to the table. The glasses were lying on top of a piece of paper containing a list of liquor and food items. I fetched the spectacles for their owner with a smile.

She laughed. "Thank you, thank you. We women are so vain, we often won't wear our glasses even if it means being half blind!"

"Not at all."

"Well, now, let me see." She peered at the photo, then shook her head. "Your photo is a bit fuzzy, Mr. Jackson. Just what am I looking at?"

I gave her the short version of the Zimbabwe Eagles tale, after which she shook her head again and handed the photo back. "A fascinating story, but I'm afraid I can't help you. I've neither seen nor heard of these birds. Are you certain they're here on the island?"

"No, I'm not."

"Because if they were, I'm sure I would know. Not much happens in the local art scene without my being aware of it, and the dealers are all aware of my interest in fine things."

"As I told you, Daniel Duarte's firm handled their sale, and Matthew may have been the principal agent in the transaction. I know that you and Matthew have done business in the past, so I had hopes that he might have mentioned the sale to you."

As I spoke, I heard the sound of a vehicle coming to a stop in front of the house.

Georgie Hall stared at me. "Who told you I did business with poor Matthew, bless his soul?"

"Apparently it's common knowledge. After all, you're a well-known collector and he was active in the sale of fine art, so a lot of people knew or at least thought they knew. I'm not exactly sure who told me first. Have I been misinformed?"

"No. No, you've not been misinformed. Ours is a gossipy little community, I'm afraid, Mr. Jackson. I do sometimes wish that people would mind their own business instead of mine, though." She sighed.

"I take it that you've learned of Matthew Duarte's death," I said.

She brightened. "Yes! Shocking! I was stunned. Dear Matthew. We were all so fond of him! A terrible accident. Terrible, terrible."

"I don't believe it was an accident," I said, watching her face carefully. "He was shot in the back of the head and the weapon wasn't in the room."

She leaned forward, wide-eyed. "How awful!" Then her brows came down. "Where did you hear that, Mr. Jackson?"

"I didn't hear it from anyone. I found the body."

"No!" She beamed at me. "Tell me everything!"

But before I could speak, there was a knock on the door.

"Damn!" she cried, glancing out the window. She climbed to her feet. "Stay right where you are, Mr. Jackson."

She went to the desk and picked up the list I'd seen there and carried it to the door, which she opened.

On the porch stood a smiling Miguel Periera holding a cardboard box piled with goods. "Good morning, Mrs. Hall. I've brought your order and come for your new shopping list, if you have one."

"I don't know what I'd do without you! You know where the kitchen is."

"Yes, ma'am." He disappeared down a hall then reappeared and accepted the new shopping list.

"Thank you, Miguel. You're a treasure!"

"My pleasure, as always, Mrs. Hall." He touched the bill of his cap and went away as Georgie Hall almost shut the door in his face and hurried back to me.

I looked out the window and saw Miguel's refrigerated van turn in the yard and drive out of my view.

"Dear Miguel," said my hostess, seating herself briskly and leaning toward me. "We'd all be in the poorhouse if it wasn't for him. Now, tell me everything about finding poor Matthew's body! How exciting! I mean, how awful!"

I gave her a stripped-down version of how I'd discovered the body.

"Dear me!" she said. "Who could have done such a thing! Poor Connie. I'll have to give her a call." She seemed to flutter without moving from her seat. "Do the police have any suspects?"

"I wouldn't know. If they don't find one soon, they'll probably want to talk with his friends, so you shouldn't be surprised to get a visit from them."

"Me?" Her hand touched her throat. "Why, I certainly can't help them."

"You may know more than you think," I said. "After all, you're a very knowledgeable member of the artistic community here on the island. A woman of your standing cannot help but know a lot about a lot of people."

"Well, yes. But I certainly don't know any murderers!"

"Sometimes a seemingly innocent piece of information turns out to be a valuable clue to investigators. For instance, had you happened to have overheard some reference to the birds I'm looking for, you might not have attached any significance to the remark, but it would have been very important to me."

"But I didn't hear any such thing."

"And that may be important in itself, since it suggests that the birds might not be on the island at all." I stood and put out my hand. "Well, thank you very much for your time. I appreciate the help you've given me. I know I can rely on your discretion to keep our conversation confidential. The fewer people who know about my inquiries, the better, as I'm sure you understand."

This last was quite the opposite of true, but I thought it would spur Georgie Hall to spread the word even faster than she might otherwise have done. The more people who knew about my search, the more likely I was to find the birds or even find a killer.

I glanced back as I went out the door. Georgie Hall was already looking at the phone.

13

Would Connie Duarte be staying in the house where her husband was murdered? I doubted it. Later, maybe, she could live there again, but not right now; not yet.

Which meant she was somewhere else.

In West Tisbury I stopped at the police station, beside the millpond. There were two swans and some ducks on the pond, and the scene looked charming and pastoral, as usual. Death has little negative effect on the beauty of nature. Given time, as the poet noted, the green grass does its work and covers even the ruins of war. Today, the ruins of Matthew Duarte were not visible.

Inside, I found the young police officer who had guarded the door of Duarte's house, and asked him if Connie Duarte was back on the island and, if so, where she was staying. She was back, but he didn't know where she was.

Any leads on the case?

I'd have to ask the chief.

Where was the chief?

Out.

A laconic cop. Or maybe, like some other cops, he just didn't like talking to me.

I drove back the way I'd come to the general store, where I used the public phone. Al Butters answered and, reluctantly, I thought, told me that Connie Duarte was staying with West Tisbury friends, Millie and Sam Hopewell. Long ago, when Al was young, Joseph McCarthy must have had quite an impact on his psyche.

The Hopewells, according to Al, lived not far from the cemetery where fans of Nancy Luce keep her grave decorated with plastic chickens. Nancy, idiosyncratic mid-nineteenth-century Vineyard citizen and author of "Poor Little Hearts," a poem mourning the death of her hens, Ada Queenie and Beauty Linna, was a better poet than many, and deserves the attention she still gets. No one, I'm sure, will leave plastic chickens on my grave.

The Hopewell house was one of those ancient farmhouses hooked to its barn by connecting sheds, such as you can still find throughout New England. I drove into the yard and stepped out to the smell of horses coming from the barn and the sound of a small dog yapping at me from a window of the house.

When I'm king of the world, I'm banning small dogs, yapping and otherwise, left turns, pay toilets, and high heels. I'm keeping fire, pestilence, war, poverty, and misery because, although they're bad, they're not as bad as the four things I'm banning.

The woman who opened the door was about my age, and was wearing loose slacks and an untucked, loose shirt, such as many broadening women wear. She had a nice round face and a pair of rimless glasses balanced on her nose. Her hair was short and tidy, with little streaks of gray mixed with the brown. The wretched little dog in her arms looked at me with angry, Napoleonic eyes.

"My name is Jackson," I said. "I'm looking for Connie Duarte."

She gave me a wary look. "Are you a friend of hers?"

"We've never met. I'm hoping she can give me some information."

"Are you a police officer?"

I considered suggesting that I was, but was sure that ploy would come back to haunt me. "I used to be."

She frowned. "You're sure you're not the police? Are you the press? Connie really isn't up to giving any interviews. She's exhausted."

"I'm sure she is," I said. "Sorrow saps our strength. I'm not with the police or the press or an insurance company. I'm one of the people who found her husband's body."

"Oh." She put a hand to her mouth. The little dog growled.

"I just need a few minutes of her time," I said. "I'm hoping she can answer the questions I was planning to ask her husband when we went to his house. I'm interested in some works of art that he may have handled."

She stroked the dog. He continued to glare at me. "Well, as far as I know, Connie didn't have much to do with Matthew's business, but wait here and I'll ask her if she's up to seeing you. You're sure you only need a few minutes?"

"Yes."

She frowned and went away, then came back. "This way, please."

I followed her down a hall and into a sitting room, where a younger woman rose from a chair. The woman had that look of fatigue that you often see on the faces of survivors.

"Connie, this is Mr. Jackson. I'll leave you two alone." She gave me a mother-hen look. "Now, don't be too long, Mr. Jackson."

"I'll be all right, Millie," said the woman. She gave me her hand as Millie Hopewell and her teeny dog left the room. "I'm Connie Duarte. Millie says you want to talk with me about some work of art my husband may have handled. I'm afraid I really don't know much about the details of his business."

I showed her the photo of the eagles, and explained what they were. "I know that Daniel Duarte's firm sold these birds, and it's possible that your husband may have been the sales agent. I'm trying to find out who bought them. Have you ever seen them or heard of them?"

She studied the photo then shook her head and handed it back to me. "I've never seen these pieces, and I don't remember any talk of them. But then, my husband never discussed much of his work with me. He said it was too boring to be the subject of conversation. I'm sorry."

"Your husband never talked about the art he bought and sold?"

"I wouldn't say never. He showed me certain pieces he was proud to handle, and spoke of others that pleased him. But he didn't speak about a lot of his work." She hesitated, then added, "Lately he was away from the house a good deal. Seeing clients, he said."

"Do you know any of their names? One of them might have purchased the eagles."

Her face was weary. "Well, I know some of the

local people. I know he sold to Georgie Hall and Gerald Jenkins. And I think Charlie Mauch bought from him. I'm sure there are records of all his clients. Sam knows more about it than I do."

"Sam?"

She looked at me with tired eyes. "Why, yes. Sam Hopewell. Millie's Sam. Sam goes in . . . went in, I suppose I should say, once a week to do Matt's books. Matt wasn't much of an accountant. Haven't you talked with Sam?"

"No, but I'd like to. Is he here?"

She shook her head. "Actually, I think he's at the office. Matt's death has left the business in limbo, just like it's left me." She touched her brow with her hand. "I'm sorry I haven't been able to help you."

"I thank you for your time," I said. "Get some rest."

I left the room and found Millie Hopewell in the kitchen. The dog was somewhere out of sight. "I need to talk with your husband," I said. "Is he at Duarte's office?"

"You seem to need to talk with a lot of people, Mr. Jackson. Sam is helping the police. Can't your questions wait?"

"A protective wife is a blessing," I said. "I won't take up much of his time. I'm looking for something Matthew Duarte may have sold. Your husband may know about it."

Her eyes drifted toward the sitting room, then came back. She picked up a dish towel and began to polish an already clean glass. "The office is in the barn behind Matthew and Connie's house. The police have asked Sam to go over Matthew's papers to see if any of his business dealings might be related to his death. An angry client, or something like that. I'm not sure he has time to see you right now."

"I'll ask him."

I drove to Matthew Duarte's house, which was still closed by yellow tape, parked, and went to the front door of the office in the barn. Today the door was unlocked and I went inside. I was in a hallway adorned with paintings. At the far end was another door. Yet another door opened from the side of the hall. I went to the closer, side door first and knocked. Nothing. I tried the knob. Locked. I went to the end of the hall and knocked on that door. A voice told me to come in.

The room was a large office decorated with small, primitive wall hangings and pieces of sculpture, and fitted with antique furniture, including two desks, each with its own computer, of course. A man was sitting behind the smaller desk. The other I took to have been Matthew Duarte's domain. There were carved oak file cases all along one wall and shelves filled with books along another. A window looked out over a green field where horses grazed. The room exuded an aura of unostentatious wealth, knowledge, and taste.

The man who stood as I came in was middle-aged, slightly bald, and dressed in old, casual clothing. He had keen eyes behind old-fashioned horn-rimmed glasses.

"You must be Mr. Jackson." He put out a strong hand and shook mine.

"Your wife called you."

"Yes. She thought I'd prefer to know who was visiting. I hope this won't take too long. The police have asked me to go over our books in hopes of finding something that might be related to Matthew's death."

"Any luck?"

He smiled slightly. "That's for the police to know, Mr. Jackson, but I don't mind telling you that so far I've found absolutely nothing out of the ordinary."

"What are you looking for?"

"I really don't know. Some unusual transaction, perhaps, or an unhappy letter indicating an angry client. The appearance or disappearance of some significant amount of money. That sort of thing, I suppose. I'm an accountant, not a policeman. I might not recognize a clue if I saw one."

"But you would recognize any unusual business record precisely because you are an accountant and not a cop."

He nodded. "Perhaps. In any case, I can give you a few minutes. What can I do for you?"

"I have two questions. The first has to do with these stone eagles." I gave him the photo and told him what I'd learned about the birds.

He held the photo up to the light from the window and nodded. "Fascinating. But if Matt had handled the sale, I'd have known about it, and the record would be in our ledgers."

He handed the photo to me. "In this business we have certain clients who don't want other people to know what they own, but in this case client confidentiality be damned. The police want to know anything that might help them."

"Most of the time, client confidentiality must make it easier to buy and sell illegal goods."

His brows came down. "I hope you're not suggesting that Matt engaged in unlawful practices."

"I'm only pointing out the obvious: that secrecy is the home of crime. Thieves hate bright lights."

"Great nations and small businesses have their secrets, too, Mr. Jackson, and they value them highly."

"I've been convinced for some time that most classified information serves to protect the asses of the people making the decisions rather than the nations or stockholders involved."

His smile came back. "You may be right, but in this case client confidentiality isn't going to protect anyone who might have wanted Matt dead. I liked Matt, and besides, I have my own reputation to protect."

"There may not be a record of the sale of the eagles, but you were close to Matthew Duarte. Have you heard any talk of them?"

He shook his head. "None. I think I would have remembered if I had."

"I seem to be at a dead end. I do have another question, though. Perhaps you can answer it: When I asked to speak to Connie Duarte, your wife asked me if I was a policeman. Why?"

He studied me, then shrugged. "It will come out eventually, I suppose. My wife considers herself to be Connie's best friend, and she wants to protect her."

"From the police? Why?"

"Because Millie thinks that Connie will be a suspect in Matthew's killing. Connie had nothing to do with it, of course. She was on Nantucket when it happened."

"Why would Connie be a suspect?" I asked, looking for confirmation of what I'd already heard.

Hopewell gave it. "Because Matthew was about to divorce her. Oh, it hadn't gotten to the lawyer stage yet, but he'd spoken of it to me, and he planned to leave her as little as he could. Matthew Duarte could be charming but you wouldn't call him a moralist."

14

Sam Hopewell glanced at his cluttered desk. It was a polite hint that I had interrupted him long enough, but I stayed and pushed him a bit.

"Are you saying that your wife thinks Connie Duarte is capable of murder?"

"Of course not. But she thinks the police might."

And she'd be right about that. The police think anyone is capable of murder.

"Did he leave a large estate?" I asked.

"Large enough, I suppose. But Connie Duarte wouldn't hurt a fly. She doesn't have a mean bone in her body, and she doesn't care about money as much as I think she should!" His eyes were hot. "Besides, she was over on Nantucket when it happened."

I wondered if his apparent anger was rooted in simple friendship with the woman, or in some deeper passion or desire. More than one man has fallen for the wife of a business partner. Then my brain did a turn and I was thinking how women, too, could be caught up in feelings for men other than their own husbands or lovers. I remembered Zee and Mahsimba arm in arm in our garden.

"Was there another woman?" I asked.

"It's all just nasty gossip," said Hopewell, making a sharp gesture. "I'll say no more about it."

But I shook my head. "You probably will say more,

actually. The police aren't fools. They're bound to learn of everything you've told me and they'll want names. It'll be in your own best interests to tell them what they want to know."

He was tired of me. "You may be right, but I'll deal with that issue when it arises, if it arises. Now, if you'll excuse me . . ."

Instead of leaving, I said, "The press will be digging around, too. The public will love a story like this: Murder and scandal on tony Martha's Vineyard. My own first guess is that the other woman is Rose Abrams."

He looked startled. "What? How did you . . . ?" Then he recovered. "What makes you think that?"

"I know she worked for Matthew Duarte and I saw her reaction when she heard of Duarte's death. She fainted, and she doesn't strike me as a woman who faints easily. Does Connie Duarte know about her?"

He drummed his fingers on his desk. "She knows there was a woman. I suspect she knows who it was. I don't like the idea of these private matters becoming public scandals. Connie deserves better than to have her name bandied about in the press."

"The more they dig, the more they'll find," I said. "They'll probably resurrect the Headless Horseman story while they're at it, since now we have two unsolved murders here in Eden."

He gave me a wary look. "There's no link between the Headless Horseman and Matthew's death. That's nonsense."

"Two killings have taken place within miles of each other on an island where murder is rare. And so far, at least, the killers are unknown. In small towns, and this island is like a small town, when a killing does happen, the cops almost always know who did it as soon as the deed is done. The state police and the press may not find any link between Duarte and the Headless Horseman, but the possibility will cross their minds, and some writer will speculate about it."

Hopewell shook his head. "No one even knows who the Headless Horseman was. Whoever he was, he certainly wasn't a Vineyarder or someone would have reported him missing. I can't imagine that what happened to him had anything to do with what happened to poor Matthew."

"You may be wrong. A man who was looking for the Zimbabwe eagles in California has been missing since just before the Headless Horseman was found. Daniel Duarte's firm sold the eagles, and Matthew may have been the agent."

He stared at me, then ran a hand over his thinning hair. "That's quite a leap in logic, isn't it? A man goes missing on one coast and his body is found three thousand miles away on another coast? Besides, Matthew wasn't the agent. If he had been, I'd have known about it."

"Maybe not. Maybe Matthew didn't let you in on all of his business arrangements. You said yourself that he wasn't a very moral man. If he was immoral in his dealings with others, maybe he was with you, too. More than one business partner has cheated another."

"I wasn't his partner, I was his accountant. If he'd sold the eagles, it would be in his books, and there's no such sale. I keep the accounts very carefully." His voice was almost pompous, but it contained that suggestion of uncertainty that you can sometimes hear beneath loud words.

"Maybe he kept another set of books," I said.

"Impossible." But he was frowning as the word was spoken.

I'd been using a lot of *maybe*s, but I tried one more. "Maybe Matthew was crookeder and smarter than you think. Isn't it possible that he was selling art objects of dubious ownership, like the eagles, or even stolen objects without your knowledge?"

"Where do you get these absurd ideas?" Hopewell walked to the door and opened it. "I'm a very busy man, Mr. Jackson. I'm afraid I can't give you any more time right now. Good-bye."

As I went out, I said, "I may want to talk with you again, Mr. Hopewell." To that he gave an abrupt nod, and shut the door.

I was hungry, but West Tisbury is a dry town, so I headed for Oak Bluffs, where you can get a beer with your lunch. In the Fireside, a popular Circuit Avenue bar of dubious reputation, I ordered a Sam Adams and a fish sandwich.

The place was pretty busy with a combination of regulars and mostly young summer people. At the back of the room Bonzo was pushing a broom, about the highest form of employment he could manage since, I'd been told, he'd blown out his brain on bad acid years before I met him. He was a sweet, dull boy who loved his mother, birds, and fishing, more or less in that order. Good old Bonzo. Too bad he didn't know anything about the Zimbabwe eagles, because I trusted him more than I trusted most of the people I'd talked to that morning.

The beer, America's finest bottled brew, was cold and good, and the fish had just enough grease in its batter to be delicious. I'd made it even better by slathering it with a thick layer of tartar sauce. Yum!

In the last few hours I'd talked with at least three people who claimed to know nothing about the eagles but who conceivably had motives to kill Matthew Duarte: Gerald Jenkins, whom Duarte had cheated out of a valuable work of art; Connie Duarte, who was about to be divorced; and Millie Hopewell, who was Connie's best friend and who might have bumped Matthew to protect Connie from being left destitute.

And Sam Hopewell could probably be added to the list because of his strong feelings about Connie. Passion has pulled many a trigger.

And while I was at it, I thought I might as well toss in Georgie Hall and Charles Mauch, because Duarte, who I knew had cheated Jenkins, might very well have dealt badly with other of his customers as well.

Everyone's a suspect but thee and me, and I'm not sure about thee.

I wondered how Mahsimba's inquiries were going and what efforts, if any, were being taken to determine whether the Headless Horseman and David Brownington were one and the same. If they were, the discovery would focus a lot of official attention on the island art scene. If they weren't, well, the Horseman would be no less identified than he was now. DNA evidence would be the best proof one way or another, but I imagined that any DNA Brownington had left behind was probably in England or Africa, in the form of a relative. A long plane flight from the body of the Headless Horseman.

Around me the voices of other diners murmured and droned through the beer- and marijuana-scented air. I doubted if any of the speakers knew or cared that there was a subsociety of artists, art dealers, and art collectors on the island, any more than most tourists were aware of the other minicultures that coexisted here: the nude bathers up in Chilmark and Aquinnah, the pond people living along the shores of the Great Ponds on the south side of the island, the fishermen who roamed the beaches in their four-by-four trucks, and the others.

The only private Vineyard society known to most of the public was that of the rich and famous summer people whose names and faces appeared in the gossip columns and on the pages of popular magazines. And I was acquainted with just enough of such people to know that public imaginings about them and their lives were none too accurate.

The more I thought of things, the more it seemed that the river of new money that was flowing over the island in an ever-widening stream had washed aside restraints that previously might have inhibited certain people from doing certain things. What once might have been unimaginable had become quite possible and attractive. A person with a wad of new bills and boundless confidence in an endless, continuing supply of the same could do almost anything: sail around the world in a small boat, buy a Vineyard mansion and tear it down and build a bigger one, climb Everest, found a college or museum, play with dynamite. Or perhaps loot a foreign land, or his own, of its ancient artifacts.

Such a person would do those things because he or she could afford to. And it might be fun.

Would some commit murder for the same reason? It was conceivable, and anything that's conceivable has probably been done.

15

Who owns history? That seemed to be the question.

I was in the Edgartown library reading about archaeological theft.

Did artifacts of past civilizations belong to the nations or people now occupying those sites, or to those individuals who found them, preserved them, and displayed them to a wider world?

And what about the damage done? Haphazard excavations often destroyed as much as they saved. Reading this, I remembered hearing my sister Margarite saying that out in the Santa Fe country where she lived, archaeologists were now being very careful about how they excavated Anasazi ruins, and were leaving many untouched, in the expectation that less destructive techniques would be developed in time.

But according to my book the ancient sites of many countries had not been dealt with so kindly. They were routinely being plundered by professional and amateur thieves, who then sold the artifacts to museums and private collectors. And since grave robbers outnumbered police throughout the world, and since there apparently was no limit to the number of collectors who were willing and able to pay top dollar for purloined art objects, it seemed equally unlikely that the theft and accompanying destruction of old sites would soon end.

Archaeologists and religious leaders were particularly outraged by such commerce, the former because the raiders destroyed sites that were often the best or only source of knowledge about ancient cultures, and the latter because the illegal commerce involved objects considered sacred: mummies, skeletons and other human remains, burial objects, and religious art.

Some American Indian tribes were demanding and receiving the return of skeletons and burial artifacts so they could be reburied with proper ritual, and according to my book the bones of at least one ninth-century Anglo-Saxon warrior had been given a Christian burial after scientists had finished their study of them. How anyone knew the warrior had been a Christian was not explained.

Political correctness, of course, often prevailed over reason. One ancient body found on the American West Coast, for instance, was not only very, very old but seemed to resemble some race other than that of American Indian. Nevertheless, over the objections of scientists intrigued by the remains' origins, it was returned by a socially sensitive federal cabinet member to a local tribe that claimed it, with little evidence, as a sacred ancestor.

By the time I put my book aside, I knew for sure that international trade in stolen artifacts was big business and that the UN's agreement to outlaw such enterprise was often ignored by the very nations that had signed the convention. There was just too much money involved, and those charged with maintaining law and order were spread too thin.

I left my book and walked outside, where North Water Street was busy with tourists, many of whom were walking in the street instead of on the sidewalk. Visitors strolling down Edgartown's streets often seem genuinely surprised when cars try to inch by them. To them the village, including its automobiles, is a make-believe place, too lovely to be real.

A catboat was beating in from the outer harbor, and the driver of the On Time ferry, recognizing the limited maneuverability of a close-hauled sailboat, held his vessel back as the catboat slid across in front of him and tacked away from the town wharf. The catboat's skipper waved thanks and the On Time continued its hundred-yard trip over to Chappaquiddick to deliver its three-car cargo.

I hadn't gone for a sail on the *Shirley J.,* our eighteen-foot Herreshoff cat, for several days, and I had a strong urge to do so now. But I only watched enviously as the catboat tacked on into the inner harbor, then I got into the Land Cruiser and drove to Aquinnah.

Joe Begay lived in Aquinnah. He and I had first met as soldiers in a faraway, long-ago war, then had met again years later when he married Toni Vanderbeck, of the Aquinnah Vanderbecks, and had left Oraibi to come and live on the island. He was a big guy with a face like granite and thick black hair that was barely beginning to gray.

In the years between our meetings, Joe had worked for some vaguely described organization in obscure places around the world. Even now, although officially retired, he occasionally went off somewhere for a few days to do some work about which he said little, if he mentioned it at all.

I had made it a point not to ask what he did or where he did it, but since our reunion I had learned that he had esoteric information about shadowy activities on several continents. And what he didn't know personally, he seemed to be able to find out. He was a handy guy to know.

His wife, Toni, sold good Native American crafts in her shop on top of the Aquinnah cliffs, the western-most point of the Vineyard, and since the summer season had already begun, I figured she'd be there and Joe would be at the house waiting for their two children to get home from school. It wouldn't be long before summer vacation and they, like my own kids, would be home all day.

I remembered how, when I was a kid, I'd looked forward to the last day of school and the feeling of freedom and endless time I'd had when that last day had come. By fall, I was ready to go back, but that first free day was like standing at the door of heaven. Now, as a parent, the thought of having my children home all day also made me as happy as I would no doubt be when they went back to school.

The Begays lived in a small, neat house not far from the beach, just north of the cliffs. There was a sandy path leading from the house to the beach. On that beach, on January 18, 1884, the frozen bodies of men, women, and children had washed ashore from the wreck of the *City of Columbus*, which had struck Devil's Bridge and sunk with a loss of 103 lives. It was the most disastrous shipwreck in Vineyard history, but today the waters smiled and twinkled under the June sun, and there were no frozen ghosts on the beach.

As I pulled into his yard, Joe Begay was sitting in

a lawn chair making a Nantucket basket. His big, thick hands looked too large for such work, but his touch was delicate and unhurried.

"I thought they made those over on that other island," I said. "You should be making Vineyard baskets."

"Actually," he said, "I believe these were first made on the Nantucket lightship, not on the island. In any case, I don't think there are any official Vineyard baskets, although I might be wrong about that. This one is going to be a genuine Native American work of art that Toni will sell for a pretty penny."

"A Native American work of art being a work of art made by a Native American, I take it."

"You bet. And you can't get any more Native American than me."

That was probably true. Joe Begay had a Navajo name, but his mother was Hopi and Joe was married to a Wampanoag. What could be more Native American than that?

"If you go into the house," Joe now said, "you should find some Ipswich Ale and a couple of glasses."

I went in and when I came back out with the ale, Joe had set his basket makings aside. I handed him a glass and took another chair and we drank. Good. God might not be a full-time brewer, but it was surely one of his trades.

"Now," said Begay, "what brings you up here to Indian country?"

"I need some help," I said. "Maybe you can give it to me."

"*Maybe* is the operational word," said Joe, taking another sip of beer. "Try me."

16

I told Joe almost everything that had happened since I'd gotten the telephone call from Stanley Crandel, omitting only whatever was going on between Zee and Mahsimba, since that whatever had nothing to do with Zimbabwe eagles, and, moreover, since I wasn't sure just what the whatever was.

When I was through, Joe said, "I've run into a few guaqueros during my travels. Most of them are just peasants trying to make a buck, but some of them are mean sons of bitches with machine guns who will kill you if you mess with them."

"I'd like to know how the system works," I said, "especially at this end of the tunnel."

"There's a lot of money at this end, but you know that already." Begay dug into his shirt pocket and got out the makings: papers and Prince Albert, just like my father used to use. He rolled a smooth cigarette and lit up. I inhaled enviously and thought, not for the first time, about taking up my bent corncob pipe again. "The system works pretty much the way you'd think it would: The locals sneak out and dig up graves or anything else that they think might contain something valuable. They sell what they find to more sophisticated types, who move it to the cities and probably sell it to somebody else, who boxes it up and calls it bananas or some other legit product, pays off anybody who needs paying off, and puts it on a ship or plane.

"They have dogs to sniff out drugs these days, but they don't have any that can sniff out ceramics or jewelry so the stuff gets to Europe or the States or wherever. It gets picked up by somebody at this end and stored away until they contact a buyer, if they don't already have one. The buyer buys and everybody in the tunnel's made some money." He blew a smoke ring that drifted east on the gentle breeze and slowly fell apart.

"There's a good market for the stuff and not much danger to people on this end, especially if there's no official report of the theft or description of what was stolen. A smart dealer will fake papers if need be, and the collector can always play innocent if anybody can actually identify some stolen object."

"No wonder business is good."

He nodded. "A lot of businesses are good when there's a ton of money lying around just asking to be spent. We have piles of it on the island these days. What do you want to know in particular?"

"Anything you can tell me about the characters in this little Vineyard drama."

"For instance?"

"For instance, Daniel Duarte and Matthew Duarte. Daniel owned the company that sold the eagles and Matthew might have handled the deal. Charles Mauch. He's a big wheel as well as a collector and he has his share of that money you were just talking about. Gerald Jenkins is another collector, but apparently one with limited funds. I'd like to know if any of their names have appeared in any official reports about this international trade in stolen objects."

"I hate to disillusion you or lose your respect, but I'm not really up to speed when it comes to this particular brand of illegal activity."

"I thought you might know somebody who is. There are a couple more names." I looked at another smoke ring floating downwind. "David Brownington and Abraham Mahsimba. Both from Zimbabwe."

He arched a brow. "I thought Mahsimba was one of the good guys. You're turning into a suspicious old man."

"All I know about this whole business is what Mahsimba has told me. And all I know about Mahsimba is what Stanley Crandel told me."

He ground the cigarette butt under his heel. "Bad habit, but I can't seem to shake it. How are Zee and the kids?"

"Zee's working and the kids are in school. I'm the only one loafing."

"Nothing new about that." We exchanged family news and a couple of fishing stories, then Begay said, "Well, I'll see what I can dig up on those names, but don't count any chickens yet."

"I won't." We shook hands and I drove home, thinking.

When I'd first taken this job, it had seemed odd to me that the eagles might have ended up on the island, of all places, but now I saw that they could be here as logically as anyplace else, since the Vineyard was home to more than its share of rich people who were collectors of fine art. If you had the money and the desire to collect artifacts, legally or illegally, why not do it here, where you lived at least part of the year, and where your privacy was enhanced by the Vineyard's long tradition of leaving its rich and famous citizens alone?

And if you were a dealer in stolen art, that same tradition would make the island an ideal location from which to do business. Your office and storage area could be in one of those large old houses at the end of a long, sandy driveway, a very private place that was almost never seen by anyone but family, friends, and hired help.

If there actually was a Vineyard trade in pilfered artifacts, it seemed it would be easy to get the merchandise to and from the island, because there were boats and planes, both private and public, coming and going every day, all year long.

But maybe not.

I wondered how I would do it if I were in the business. Could I tie up my own boat to some dock and load or unload freight without eventually attracting unwanted attention? Would anyone wonder about the crates and bundles I loaded or unloaded from my plane?

Would it be better to use legitimate freight services like UPS or FedEx? They could deliver almost anything almost anywhere, and were extremely dependable.

I remembered reading about some great diamond, the Cullinan, perhaps, being shipped from South Africa to England for cutting. To deceive would-be thieves, much publicity had been devoted to a special ship that would carry the stone north, but it had actually been sent in a small box by regular post since the royal mail was such a dependable carrier.

Maybe I would use the U.S. mail to transport my purloined artifacts.

Maybe I could just drive my own van back and forth from the mainland. Why not? If I mixed legitimate art sales with illegal ones, no one would think much about my coming and going.

Had Matthew Duarte owned a van? I hadn't seen one, but maybe it was parked in his barn beside the climate-controlled room that held his art objects until they could be sold.

At the end of our driveway I checked the mailbox. Empty. Curious, because in this age of endless catalogs, we always get junk mail if nothing else. I went down our driveway and found the reason why: Zee's little Jeep was parked in the yard. She'd come home early from the hospital. Curious again, because Zee, a dedicated healer, almost never came home early.

I parked and stepped out and immediately heard voices from the gardens beyond the porch. Zee's and another I thought I knew. I went and saw that I was right. Mahsimba and Zee were standing amid the raised beds, wineglasses in their hands, talking and laughing.

Zee saw me and waved, and Mahsimba turned and looked at me with his deep, golden eyes.

"Get yourself a beer and join us," Zee called. "I'm giving Mahsimba another guided tour of our vegetables and flowers."

I nodded and went into the house, where I took my time pouring myself a Sam Adams before carrying my mug back outside.

"You're home early," I said to Zee.

"Mahsimba finished his gallery visits earlier than we expected, so I brought him home for a drink before the kids get out of school."

"I didn't know you were working together," I said. "I thought you were at the hospital."

"Your wife has been kind enough to be my driver this afternoon," said Mahsimba. "She has been a great help, since I must consult maps to find my way about your island. Because of her assistance, I believe I've now visited every gallery that is open."

"I took the afternoon off," said Zee in a delicate voice. "Mattie and John were both busy, so I stood in."

I looked at Mahsimba. "Have you learned anything useful?"

He made a small gesture with his free hand. "I've found that there is a good market for art, and that much of what is for sale is of quite high quality, including objects from abroad. There is also a considerable market for antiques, again including objects from abroad. Your small island is quite a sophisticated place, I find."

"We also have some people who've never been as far as Nantucket, and others who can barely read."

He nodded. "That is the case in all communities. But I don't think that those citizens are central to my inquiries. The others—the wealthy, the well traveled, the educated—those are the people of interest to me. The eagles I seek will not be found in the home of a poor or ignorant man or woman. They will be found in some great house or museum." He sipped his wine and Zee's eyes followed his hand while it plucked a weed from a flower box. Then his eyes rose to mine. "And how have your investigations gone, J.W.? Have you learned anything of interest?"

"I've learned some things. Whether they have anything to do with the eagles remains to be seen."

"Tell me."

So I told him about everything except my visit to Joe Begay. I don't tell anybody everything.

17

By the time I finished my narrative, we were sitting on the balcony, looking out over the yard and gardens toward the barrier beach on the far side of Sengekontacket Pond.

"You seem to have covered a lot of ground in a single day," said Zee.

"There's more to cover."

Mahsimba's voice was rich and melodious. "You have spoken to three people whose names I've heard in my own inquiries: Mauch, Hall, and Jenkins. They seem to be well known to the owners and managers of the galleries I've been visiting. Perhaps I should speak with them myself."

"Perhaps you should. You know a lot more about this matter than I do." As I spoke I heard the faint running-brook sound of children's voices and laughter. Joshua and Diana had gotten off their school bus and were coming down the driveway. As I rose, I said to Mahsimba, "If you like, you can use our phone to call them right now. Then, tomorrow, if they're willing to meet with you, I'll take you to them." I looked at Zee. "I'll go down and meet the kids. You two finish your drinks."

Without waiting for a reply I went down the stairs.

"Hi, Pa!"

"How was school?"

"It was okay."

"Did you read?"

"Yes. Pa, we're hungry."

We went inside and I set milk and oatmeal cookies on the table. They dropped their backpacks and climbed into chairs.

"Pa?"

"What?"

"Can we have a dog?"

"No. No dogs. We have cats. Oliver Underfoot and Velcro."

"A puppy almost followed me home today. If he follows me home again, can we keep him?"

"No. If he follows you home, he'll follow me right to the dog pound."

"What's a dog pound, Pa?"

"It's a jail for dogs."

"All our friends have dogs."

"Good. You can play with their dogs."

Zee and Mahsimba came in.

"Ma?"

"What, sweetie?"

"Can we have a dog?"

"Ah, the old play-the-parents-against-each-other trick, eh? What did your father say?"

"He said the puppy would go to jail."

"What puppy?" She gave them a skeptical look. "Not one that followed you home, I suppose?"

The children exchanged glances and chewed their cookies.

"One that almost followed them home today and might follow them home later," I said.

"Oh, that puppy," said Zee. "Well, you know how your father feels about dogs."

"In my country," said Mahsimba, "some people eat dogs. They say it's very good meat."

Joshua and Diana stared at him with big eyes. "They eat puppies?"

Mahsimba nodded solemnly. "I do not eat them myself, you understand, but others do. Is that why you want a dog? To eat it?"

"No!"

I rubbed my chin. "Maybe I've been wrong, kids. Maybe we should get a dog. I like to cook."

"No!" Diana shook her little head. "You can't cook our dog, Pa!"

"Just to be sure, we probably shouldn't have any dog at all."

It was an ongoing issue in our house. My position was that people who own dogs are slaves to animals who also want to be slaves. If you have a dog, you have to walk it, feed it, clean up after it, and allow yourself to be slathered by a creature that only wants to know what it can do for you. I prefer cats, who don't care what you want unless it gets them what they want. When it came to dogs, I considered myself an abolitionist. No slaves for me. No being a slave, either.

"Your father is only joking about eating dogs," said Zee, giving me a hard look.

"Is that right, Pa?"

"Well, maybe. But Mahsimba wasn't joking. Were you, Mahsimba?"

"No, indeed," said Mahsimba.

"So," I said, "we're agreed, then. No dogs."

The children chewed.

"Pa?"

"What?"

"Can we have a ferret?"

"No! No ferrets. They eat ferrets in Africa, you know."

Diana looked at Mahsimba, but before she could speak, he said, "You mentioned that I might use your telephone, J.W."

"If you use the one in the bedroom, you'll have some privacy."

"Right through that door," said Zee, pointing.

The children studied me carefully.

"No ferrets," I said again.

They chewed their cookies and exchanged glances. It's not easy being the children of a tyrant.

When Mahsimba came from the bedroom, the children were out in the yard, playing in the slanting afternoon light, and I was in Archie Bunker's chair reading Blake's poetry and wondering once again whether I was getting it. With Blake it's hard to tell. Zee came out of the kitchen.

"I have spoken with Charles Mauch, Mrs. Hall, and Gerald Jenkins," said Mahsimba, "and they have agreed to meet with me tomorrow morning." He paused, then added with a small smile, "It was not my impression that they were all eager to do so."

"Mahsimba, you must join us for supper," said Zee, lifting her chin a bit as she glanced at me.

"Good idea," I said. "I'll give Mattie a call and tell her we've stolen you for the evening. I'll drive you over to John and Mattie's place after we eat and pick you up there in the morning."

"I'm delighted to accept your invitation." Mahsimba inclined his head and straightened again. He turned to Zee. "May I assist you in the kitchen, Zeolinda?"

"No, you may not," I said, putting my book aside and standing up. "Because I'm the cook. The two of you can go back to the balcony and admire the sunset. I'll call you when the food is ready."

Zee gave me a curious, dreamy look as they carried their drinks up the stairs. While I cooked I could hear the faint sounds of their voices and laughter.

The next morning when I got to John and Mattie's place to pick up Mahsimba, Mattie ushered me back out onto the porch while Mahsimba was carrying his coffee cup to the sink. She looked up at me with guarded eyes.

"I think your wife may be slightly smitten with our guest."

I said nothing.

"He's handsome and exotic," said Mattie, glancing back into the house. "I doubt if she's ever met anyone like him."

"She's never met anyone like me, either," I said, putting on a smile.

"I'm serious, J.W." She placed a hand on my arm. "I know it's probably none of my business, but I thought I should tell you. It worries me."

"Thanks."

"She was moody even before he came."

"I know."

"I—" She broke off as Mahsimba came out the door, then went on. "I . . . I hope you learn something useful today, so you can both get back to your normal lives."

Return to Normalcy. Wasn't that Harding's promise to America?

"It is a worthy hope," said Mahsimba, "and one I share."

We climbed into the Land Cruiser.

"Do you have a schedule," I asked, "or do we just visit these people as we come to them?"

"Mr. Mauch has agreed to meet me at nine, Mrs. Hall at ten, and Mr. Jenkins said he'd be at home all day."

As we drove toward Vineyard Haven, I said, "I'll go in with you if you wish, or I can stay in the car. You might learn more if you're alone. Mauch was not too pleased with me."

"Ah, yes. He blamed you for distressing the woman, as I recall. Rose Abrams; was that her name?"

"Yes."

"Let us hope that Miss Abrams has recovered by now. I'd like to have you come in with me, if you are willing and if Mr. Mauch has no objections, so you can compare what you saw and heard before with what you see and hear today."

"Fine. I'll go in and if Mauch objects, I'll go out again."

As it turned out, Mauch frowned but didn't object, and I followed him and Mahsimba down the art-filled corridor to his office. Nothing, including Mauch, looked different than it had the day before.

The other two sat in crested leather chairs, and I took a smaller seat to one side.

Mauch looked at Mahsimba. "I don't know what I can tell you that I didn't tell Mr. Jackson yesterday."

Mahsimba's eyes had been taking in the room's adornments but now met Mauch's. He smiled. "Well, sir, your name interests me. Are you by any chance a descendant of the Carl Mauch who first published descriptions of Great Zimbabwe back in the 1870s?"

Mauch leaned back. "As a matter of fact, he was

my great-grandfather. You are one of the few who has made that link. You know your country's history, obviously."

"And would I be amiss to presume that your interest in the art of ancient cultures may be a continuance of your family's interests since Carl Mauch's time?"

Mauch nodded. "You would not be amiss. I should tell you, however, that my great-grandfather's theories about the origins of Great Zimbabwe are not shared by me. I do not, for instance, subscribe to the notion that the place was built by the Phoenicians, or that the wood used for the lintels was imported from the Queen of Sheba." He allowed himself a smile.

Mahsimba returned it. "Your knowledge of the ruins is clearly considerable, so you are, of course, familiar with the Zimbabwe eagles. That gives me hope that you may be of real assistance to me."

Mauch glanced at me. "I regret to tell you that you're mistaken. As I told Mr. Jackson yesterday, I am not a specialist in African art, and I've neither seen nor heard anything about the eagles. I recommended that he speak with Mr. and Mrs. Butters and Matthew Duarte." He hesitated. "That was before I knew of Matthew's death, of course."

"Of course. You also spoke with Mr. Jackson about the international trade in stolen art. Are you familiar with any such trade existing here on Martha's Vineyard?"

Mauch tapped a finger against the leather arm of his chair. Then he shook his head. "I know of none." His brief smile had gone away. "There are rumors, of course, but I don't believe I'll pass them along. It's all idle gossip."

Mahsimba nodded understandingly. "Such gossip can be both ugly and wrong. Naturally you don't want to be a part of it. Let me change the subject. As a collector yourself, and an expert in your field, tell me: Would the seller of artwork that might have been illegally obtained from ancient sites have to be very discreet about peddling his wares? Or could he be fairly open about it?"

"That," said Mauch, "would depend entirely upon the object in question. Only a very few collectors would knowingly purchase art that they knew had been stolen, such as that taken from Jews by the Nazis, for instance. On the other hand, all but the most culturally sensitive of collectors would probably feel free to buy an object that had no pedigree, even though they might suspect that it was loot from some unauthorized dig. Private collections and even great museums are full of such objects."

"Including yours?" I asked.

Mauch surprised me by not getting angry. Instead he smiled and nodded.

"Even mine," he agreed. "I have some Mayan pieces that came into my possession from private dealers who could not authenticate their origins. I treasure them, but I assure you that if they are ever proven to have been stolen, I will immediately return them to their proper owners."

"And what's the likelihood of that happening?"

His smile grew broader and more ironic. "Very slight. Very, very slight. And until it happens, I consider them my personal property, honestly and honorably purchased."

"Will you give me the names of those dealers?" asked Mahsimba.

"You will forgive me if I do not," said Mauch. "I view them as honest men, and I don't approve of bringing grief to honest men."

"I understand perfectly," said Mahsimba. "Perhaps you can tell me less than their names. Are any of them living here on Martha's Vineyard?"

Mauch took time to answer. Then he shook his head. "No," he said. "One used to live here, but he's here no longer."

"Do you know where he is?"

Mauch shook his head. "He has, ah, departed the island. Where he's gone I cannot say."

18

"He told you more than he told me," I said to Mahsimba as we drove out of Vineyard Haven and headed up-island along State Road. "When I talked with him he never indicated that he knew much about Great Zimbabwe, only that he was aware of the eagles in the museums. You got him to admit that he knew a lot more than just that."

"You were once a police officer, J.W. You know that people will sometimes give you information only if you ask the right question."

True. I wished I'd thought to ask the Carl Mauch question, but I hadn't. Maybe my brain was wearing out. Maybe I was an early Alzheimer's victim. Had I grown old? Was it time to wear my trousers rolled?

"You should ask Georgie Hall about illegal art sales," I said. "Mauch might shun gossip, but I don't think Georgie Hall will. Unless it applies to her, that is."

"Do you think Mrs. Hall would buy illegally obtained works of art?"

"Mauch seemed to think a lot of people will if there isn't a paper trail identifying the objects as stolen. I know that Georgie Hall is not above a deal from the bottom of the deck. She and Matthew Duarte were glad to pull a fast one on Gerald Jenkins."

"I believe you said that Jenkins has less money

than Mauch or Hall, and that his collection is smaller."

"Yes. African art is his specialty, and he recognized the eagles in the photo I showed him. He said he'd heard nothing about them being on the Vineyard, and I think he would have had them on display if he'd had them. He likes to have his stuff out where he can see it. My impression was that he'd love to have them, but probably wouldn't have had the money to buy them if and when they passed through Daniel Duarte's hands."

"It is possible that his anger at Matthew Duarte and Mrs. Hall might lead him to tell us something we might otherwise not learn."

"Yes, that's possible, but he was pretty careful about his comments when I talked with him."

Mahsimba nodded. "First we will see what Mrs. Hall can tell us." He looked about him. "Your island is very lovely. These stone walls are similar to some I've seen in Britain."

"Another reason why they call it New England."

We came into North Tisbury, passed the great oak, and took North Road on toward Menemsha. At Tea Lane I took a left, then another one into Georgie Hall's driveway. The sight of her huge new house caused Mahsimba's brow to rise and his lips to curve up fleetingly.

Georgie Hall was all wide smiles when she opened the door. She grasped Mahsimba's hand warmly, and was delighted to see me again.

"My husband tells me that your friend Mr. Crandel is a man of considerable means and that his family has been on the island for generations! How splendid. Do come in."

Green is a hue that unites folks of many skin tones. We followed Georgie into her house beautiful until she waved us into the same overstuffed chairs in which she and I had seated ourselves when last we had talked.

"Ah," said Mahsimba, eyeing the niche in the far wall, "my friend Mr. Jackson did not exaggerate your excellent taste in art, Mrs. Hall. I believe your Bakuba portrait sculpture is as fine as any I've seen in the British Museum."

"Oh, thank you, Mr. Mahsimba. Coming from an African that is high praise indeed." She arranged herself in her chair. "Now, gentlemen, how may I be of use to you?"

Mahsimba spread his graceful hands. "If time allowed, Mrs. Hall, it would be my greatest pleasure to ask for a tour of your wonderful house. Alas, Marvell's winged chariot is at our back, so I must forgo that delight." He leaned back in his chair. "Instead, I hope you will allow me to take advantage of what Mr. Jackson has characterized as your extensive knowledge of your island's artistic society."

Her pink mouth kinked up at its ends and a plump hand fluttered. "Oh, my," she said, "I wouldn't think of myself in that way."

Mahsimba's smile was elegant. "You are too modest, madame. I have visited many galleries since my arrival here, and your name and intelligence have been remarked upon wherever I have gone."

She beamed. "How charming of you to inform me, Mr. Mahsimba. I suppose I do have some knowledge of the Vineyard's artists and collectors."

"I have been assured," said Mahsimba, "that you are not only familiar with all public matters, but that many individuals confide their most private hopes and fears to you, sure in the knowledge that such confidences are completely secure. Such a reputation is enviable and rare."

"You are too, too kind!"

"And too admiring, I assure you, to ask you to reveal any of those confidences. However, I am bold enough to hope that you will speak to me on an issue of public concern. To be precise, I am interested in your views on the possibility of illegal art sales taking place right here on your lovely island." He raised a graceful hand. "Of course, I know that a woman of your ethical standards would be the first to condemn such activity. But often it cannot be proved, and there are only rumors of such deeds.

"Your reputation for keenness of observation, intelligence, and unbending honesty have brought me to your door in hopes that some breath, some faint wind might have carried such rumors to your ears. If so, I dare hope that you will reveal them to me, and that the ten thousand miles I have traveled to your door will not have been traveled in vain."

"Ten thousand miles! My!" Georgie Hall's hand lifted to her throat as she gazed at her exotic visitor. I gazed at him too, wondering how much I might also be bamboozled by his charm.

Our hostess made her decision. She leaned forward, eyes bright. "Now, I am certainly not one to spread gossip," she said, "but I have heard . . . things."

"Things?" Mahsimba's voice became as secretive as hers.

"Well! I would be the last one to speak ill of the dead, but Matthew Duarte was not above committing, shall we say, questionable business acts. He knew everyone, of course, and certain people who had frequent dealings with him have come into possession of objects that I, for one, rather doubt they came by totally honestly."

"Ah!" Mahsimba frowned conspiratorially and leaned closer. "Yes, I've heard certain names."

"Gerald Jenkins? Am I right?" Her voice was eager, her eyes were bright.

Mahsimba said nothing, but beamed at her and leaned back in his chair.

"I knew it!" exclaimed his hostess. "And to be frank I've had my suspicions of Charles Mauch, too, however respectable he may seem!"

Mahsimba looked at her admiringly. "You are as keen as you are modest, Mrs. Hall. I also have it on good authority that Mr. Mauch may have certain items of questionable origins in his collection."

Georgie Hall could not have looked more pleased. "I'm not surprised, Mr. Mahsimba. Some people have much more money than character, sad to say."

"How true; how sad but true. Have you ever heard anything about how these dubious items are transported to or from the island?"

Georgie Hall sighed. "I'm sorry to say that I can't be of help to you in that area. I don't know anyone in the transportation field, I'm afraid." Her brow furrowed. "By sea or air, I would guess."

And an excellent guess it was, I thought, since those were the only ways to get to the island.

"I'm sure you're correct," said Mahsimba. "To continue my poor metaphor, have any other names floated by on the wind?"

"Well, the Butterses have a small collection, of

course, but I believe they brought most of their items with them when they returned from Africa." She examined her perfect nails. "I don't really know them well, I'm afraid, though I do see them occasionally at openings and parties."

"Has Samuel Hopewell's name been mentioned?"

She gave an audible sniff. "Samuel Hopewell? Samuel Hopewell is merely Matthew Duarte's accountant. To my knowledge, he knows nothing at all about art. Certainly I've never heard him mentioned with regard to anything remotely aesthetic."

So much for Samuel Hopewell. Mahsimba glanced at his watch and flowed to his feet. "You've been more than generous with your valuable time, Mrs. Hall, and even if other duties weren't calling us, we would be amiss to take further advantage of you. I thank you a thousand times for your kind assistance."

As we left he repeatedly admired her and her house, and by the time she had waved good-bye from her porch, she had invited him, but not me, to a small gathering at her home the following weekend.

As we drove away, Mahsimba allowed himself a sustained smile. "Well, J.W.," he said. "What did you make of Mrs. Hall's contribution to our quest?"

"Her dismissal of Sam Hopewell as anyone involved in the illegal sales of art makes him an immediate suspect."

"She was right about Mauch."

"True. Of course, she didn't include herself as the benefactor of shady practices."

"You speak of the Bakuba head. Yes, there is that. But she probably sees that purchase as a sharp business success rather than as an immoral act. Women such as Mrs. Hall only accept themselves as wicked when their questionable activities are clothed in romance. Simple theft, even of a Bakuba portrait, lacks the glamour necessary to make it acceptably amoral."

I drove toward Gerald Jenkins's house. "When you're through here," I said, "would you mind having a talk with Sam Hopewell? He should be in Duarte's office."

Mahsimba glanced at me. "Because Mrs. Hall's certainty that he knows nothing about art, stolen or otherwise, makes you sure that he does?"

"Not so much that as the fact that I'd like to get into the barn where Duarte stored his artwork before selling it. I presume there's an alarm system and that it can be turned off or on from the office. I'd like to know where the switch is. Maybe while you and Hopewell talk, I can spot it. I should have done that when I was there before, but I didn't."

"Perhaps I should just ask Mr. Hopewell to show us the room."

"If he will, it'll save me some work."

"Have you always had criminal impulses, J.W.?"

An interesting question. After a while, I said, "Well, I can still remember stealing a piece of candy from the paper store when I was five. My father made me put it back and apologize to Mr. Irving. Since then I've broken all of the Commandments at one time or another."

To my surprise he made no saucy retort, but only nodded and after a pause said, "Yes. Many of us have."

19

Gerald Jenkins and Mahsimba had conversed for no more than five minutes before some sort of mutual recognition passed between them and I found myself following them on a tour of Jenkins's house, listening to the two of them comment on his collection of Africana. It was as though they were old friends meeting after years of separation. We passed from room to room as they studied and critiqued sculptures, baskets, ceramics, carvings, paintings, weapons, jewelry, tools, and utensils. Jenkins was the proud but modest owner and Mahsimba was the knowledgeable, admiring guest. I was ignored.

Jenkins showed us no soapstone eagles, but when we returned to his studio he was more than willing to talk about them and express the hope that if we ever located them he'd be allowed to make a bid for them, however unlikely it was that he could afford the purchase. As we left, Mahsimba received an invitation to return soon. It was his second such invitation of the day. In the invitation tourney, it was Mahsimba two, Jackson zero.

As we drove toward West Tisbury, Mahsimba said, "Well?"

"You got the grand tour. That was more than I got."

"He has a very fine collection. Small but elegant. I must admit that I like him."

"I do too. I hope it's not clouding my vision."

He nodded. "A warm heart is important in love, but a cool head is better in this sort of work."

The old conundrum emerged into my consciousness: Which is best? Cold heart and hot head, cold heart and cold head, hot heart and cold head, or hot heart and hot head? Or should we avoid the extremes of hot and cold, and deal only with warm and cool? What would Socrates say? Or Nietzsche? Or Archy and Mehitabel?

"While you were getting the tour," I said, "I tried to estimate where, if anywhere, he might have a secret room for his special treasures. I couldn't fit one inside the house, but maybe he has one in the basement."

"It is possible," said Mahsimba, "but my impression of Gerald Jenkins is that he displays his favorite objects."

"Yes."

In Duarte's office, Hopewell was looking more rumpled than when last I'd seen him. His desk was cluttered with ledgers and papers, and his computer screen was filled with numbers. My presence did not please him but he tolerated me when I took a seat at the side of the room and left him and Mahsimba more or less alone together at his desk.

Hopewell's fingers danced impatiently over some papers until, seemingly noticing them at their work, he placed them flat on the desk. "So you're from Zimbabwe, eh? I'm afraid I have to admit that I don't know where that is, except that it's in Africa somewhere. When I grew up we had the Belgian

Congo and South Africa and those are about the only countries I can remember being south of the equator. Geography was never my strong point."

Mahsimba gave no sign of offense. "The country that was Southern Rhodesia when you were in school is now Zimbabwe. We are bounded by Zambia on the north, Mozambique on the east, Botswana on the west, and South Africa to the south."

"It's all pretty confusing," said Hopewell. "All these new countries in Africa and Asia. I can't keep up with them. Sorry."

"No need to apologize, I'm often confused myself." Mahsimba smiled the smile I was beginning to recognize as a calculated and effective diplomatic tool. "I take it, Mr. Hopewell, that you are not a great traveler."

"Good Lord, no! America is good enough for me, and I'm not interested in much of that either! No, New England is more than big enough for me. In fact, I'd be hard-pressed to think of any reason to leave the Vineyard. Why go somewhere else when everything you like is right here? You know what I mean?"

Mahsimba smiled the smile. "I'm sure many people share your view. Did your late partner share your reluctance to leave your lovely island?"

"If anything, he was worse. He hated to travel and only did it if it was absolutely unavoidable and if it was within the forty-eight states. He wouldn't even go to Canada! He disliked any food he hadn't tasted in his mother's kitchen, and he loathed the idea of having to learn foreign customs. I believe it was in part our shared dislike of travel that made our relationship as pleasant as it was. Whatever happened on the TV news, we were right here on Martha's Vineyard, the best place in the world."

"I would have imagined that dealers in international art would have to make frequent trips to foreign lands in search of new acquisitions."

"Not necessary these days, Mr. Mahsimba." Hopewell gestured first toward his computer and then toward the crowded shelves around the room. "Everything is on the Net or between covers. Matthew could bid, buy, and sell anywhere in the world without leaving this office. It's an electronic age."

"And once you've made your purchases and sales, may I ask how your goods are transported to and from the island?"

Hopewell shrugged. "By the usual means. Usually professional shipping companies, sometimes special couriers."

"One would think being on a small island would complicate your business dealings."

Hopewell allowed himself a smile. "If the Vineyard was a poverty-stricken pile of sand, that might be the case, but this little island is wallowing in money and people looking for ways to spend it. Any difficulties Matthew might have had transporting his merchandise were more than compensated for by his proximity to customers anxious to buy what he had to sell." His voice became cynical. "Matthew sold them goods that allowed them to see themselves as sophisticated, not just rich. There's always a market for such items."

While he spoke, I let my eyes roam the office, taking in the door and windows and lingering on Matthew Duarte's desk, whence, I noted, an electric wire led unobtrusively beneath an Oriental rug and disappeared into an inner wall. When Hopewell made his last remark, I looked at him with unexpected appreciation. He seemed less inclined than many people to rationalize his work.

"Your desk suggests that you are a man of business as much as a man of art," Mahsimba was saying.

"Only a man of business," replied Hopewell. "Matthew handled the art. Oh, I know what I like, but I've often been advised to keep my artistic opinions to myself and I've been smart enough to do just that. No, I handle the dollars and cents and that's all. Matthew, God bless him, was smart enough to let me do it because he had no head for figures and knew it. We were a good team."

"And now that he's gone?"

Hopewell's face took on the expression of an unhappy man. "I don't know. I can't run the business myself because I know nothing about our product. I suppose Connie will either find a new partner who does or will sell the firm. But before she does that, I have to make sure the books are in shape. And as Mr. Jackson there may have told you, the police have asked me to search back for any sale or transaction that might have incited someone to shoot poor Matthew. That's what this chaos is all about." He gestured at the piles of paper and ledgers.

"And have you found anything?"

Hopewell was suddenly wary. "As I told Mr. Jackson before, I'm afraid that's between me and the police."

Mahsimba again smiled the smile. "Of course. I can only encourage you to work closely with the authorities. Am I correct in assuming that all of Mr. Duarte's business transactions are recorded in these files?"

But Hopewell had become a more careful witness. "Of course. Now if you'll excuse me, I have work to do."

Mahsimba rose from his chair. "You've been most generous with your time. One last question: Are you aware of rumors about traffic in unauthorized international art here on the island?"

Hopewell, too, was on his feet. "I pay little attention to rumors, sir. I only know that this business was engaged in no such traffic."

"I understand," said Mahsimba, "that Matthew Duarte constructed a room here in this barn where he kept art he'd not yet sold. Would it be possible for me to look at that room?"

Hopewell came around the desk and opened the office door. "No, sir, it would not. I must make an inventory of the contents before anyone but the police will be allowed to enter. I wish you good day."

"And good day to you. My thanks for your time and assistance." Mahsimba walked past Hopewell with me in his wake. The door closed firmly behind us and I heard the click of a lock. Hopewell was tired of visitors.

As we drove back to Edgartown, Mahsimba was thoughtful. I was thinking about what I'd seen while listening with half an ear to what he and Hopewell had said.

"It is interesting, is it not," said Mahsimba, "that an art dealer would shun travel to the places where his goods might be found?"

"Maybe Hopewell is right about computers and

publications. Maybe you can learn all you need to know without leaving home."

"Possibly. I would think, though, that before spending a great deal of money to buy an art object, one would want to examine it carefully, in person."

"There are probably experts in every country who will work as agents."

"Yes, that seems probable. Still, if I were paying a huge sum for an object, or if I heard about some collection of objects that were of interest to me, I think I'd want to see the goods myself before bidding. Matthew Duarte was an art expert. It's a curiosity to me that he never went abroad. He must have trusted his agents completely."

I stirred the pot: "And there's the matter of illegal artworks coming into the States. Even if legally traded art can be bought and sold via computers, is the same true of illegal art? You might be able to get your European expert on medieval art to take a look at the latest silver chalice for you and e-mail you a picture of it via satellite, but can you do the same thing with, say, a stolen statue from an Indonesian temple? Do art thieves use computers to show their wares to prospective buyers? Are there experts for hire who will authenticate the value of stolen art objects?"

Mahsimba stared ahead. "Modern technologies are as available to criminals as to anyone else, and experts can be bribed."

Where there is a lot of money lying around, people who wouldn't think of robbing you personally will be glad to pick up the wealth. I remembered a news story about an armored car that somehow managed to spill several bags of money as it traveled through a poor neighborhood. The money in the street simply disappeared, except for a fifty-cent piece that was turned in by a young boy. The authorities couldn't understand why other people didn't turn in the money they had found. They were the only ones who were perplexed.

"I've read that policing the exchange of electronic information is getting more complicated every day," I said. "As fast as the computer cops come up with a way to keep things honest, the crooks come up with new ways to beat the system."

"John Skye has a computer in his office," said Mahsimba. "If he will allow me to do so, I'll spend some time with it and see if I can discover anything useful."

"You're on your own," I said. "I know absolutely nothing about computers."

He smiled. "When your children are a bit older, they will no doubt be able to teach you."

"No doubt."

"Does Samuel Hopewell strike you as an honest man?"

I thought for a moment. "Yes. But Ananias might well have fooled me."

He nodded. "Yes, and not only you. Still, Hopewell struck me, too, as a man whose tongue was not forked."

I left Mahsimba at the Skyes' farm and drove home alone. I was full of thoughts and anxious for night to fall. As I turned into my driveway, one of my front wheels spun a rock up into my windshield. It smacked against the glass and left a small hole just under my rearview mirror.

Blast and drat. I drove down to the house, parked, and looked at the hole again. This time it didn't look like something done by a rock. It looked like a bullet hole. I felt a sudden chill and looked up the driveway toward the road. No shooter was coming for a second try.

I went inside the house and got my old police .38 revolver, then went through the trees up to the end of my drive, moving carefully, as I'd been taught to move long ago when the army was trying to make a warrior of me.

The closer I got to the road, the slower I moved. I saw no one. I went to the place where the shot must have come from. Nothing. Whoever had been there was gone.

I walked back to the truck and examined the inside. There, buried in the cracked backrest of the front seat I found the slug. It looked like a .38 or a 9mm. A pistoleer had been at work. Had he been a rifleman, I'd probably be dead.

I was shaking. I went inside and put my revolver away and gradually got my nerves under control.

Just before the children got home from school, the phone rang and I jumped to my feet as though I'd heard another gun go off. I took a deep breath and picked up the receiver. The caller was Joe Begay.

"I've been digging around, and I've come up with some information that might interest you. It's about two guys named Mahsimba and Brownington."

20

"First some background," said Begay. "There's a UNESCO convention that makes it illegal to sell anything considered a cultural treasure."

I made myself listen. "I heard about it."

"Then you also probably heard that a lot of countries don't pay much attention to it, or to other international laws prohibiting such trade. The United States has laws of its own that supposedly have stopped such trade here, but of course they haven't."

"You're becoming a cynical old man, Sarge."

"I prefer to think of myself as skeptically middle-aged. Do you want me to go on, or do you just want to be snotty to your elders?"

"I always treat the aged and infirm with respect. What about Mahsimba?"

"There's a guy named Abraham Mahsimba who sometimes works with the UN, trying to enforce the UNESCO convention. It's a little unclear whether he really works for Interpol. He did once, but if he still does, he's on a leave of absence of some kind and is working by himself. Sometimes these lines get fuzzy."

Begay worked within just such fuzzy lines, I suspected. "Go on," I said.

"My sources say he's interested in a onetime colleague of his named David Brownington, who may be working for the other side. Brownington is a

Zimbabwean of British descent. His parents were farmers back when Zimbabwe was Southern Rhodesia. He and Mahsimba didn't know each other back home, but they met at Oxford and hit it off. They both went to work for Interpol in cooperation with the UN efforts to stop the international trade in art objects.

"Brownington was good at his work, but apparently a time came when there was more money to be made in the business he was hired to stop than in trying to stop it, and he went over."

It was not an unfamiliar tale. Cops are constantly exposed to the possibility of graft and corruption, since their work puts them in regular contact with criminals, many of whom have more money than the cops do, and many of whom are willing to share envelopes of cash with policemen who will shut their eyes under certain circumstances. Most bribed cops have a limit to what they'll ignore, but some use the gun and the shield to commit or abet major-league crimes. A rogue cop can be very dangerous, indeed, and all too often is protected by the code of silence adhered to by even honest policemen and police unions.

Begay went on. "Brownington played both sides for a while, according to my people. He helped break up some sales rings, but took money to ignore others. He needed the money to put his sister's kids through some pricey public schools in England, if that motive strikes you as important."

"Crooks have families just like everybody else," I said.

"Yeah. Well, to bring this business up-to-date, Mahsimba began to think his friend Brownington might not be playing with a straight deck and told him so, so Brownington could resign before he got fired or arrested. Brownington resigned."

"And went to work for the other guys."

"Nothing quite as overt as that. He created a company called Brownington Limited and became a consultant."

A consultant. It had once been my idea of the perfect job. People pay you for advice whether they take it or not and whether it's any good or not. "To whom?" I asked.

"To anyone who wanted to hire him. He had a lot to sell: thorough knowledge of the UN's operations against the trade in artifacts and of Interpol's operations, too, and thorough knowledge of how the artifact trade worked best or worst. And, to boot, he was also well trained in paramilitary operations."

"Just the kind of guy to give wise advice or assistance to exporters of purloined cultural artifacts."

"And to honest dealers who might want to know the best way to acquire or ship legitimate goods to legitimate buyers. In a lot of countries, what Americans call graft is considered a normal cost of doing business. Before transactions can take place, money has to change hands. Brownington knew who to pay and how much, and thereby could get things done fast, efficiently, and legally."

"A handy guy to know. Why is Mahsimba after him?"

"You'll have to ask Mr. Mahsimba."

I would do that. "What about the other names I gave you? Were you able to get lines on any of them?"

"You can find out about Mauch in *Who's Who*. He

travels all over the world giving lectures and is considered the final word with regard to Central and South American antiquities in particular. I couldn't find anything about Jenkins aside from the fact that he's a buyer with good taste and a relatively limited wallet."

"What about the Duartes? They seem to be in the middle of whatever's going on here."

"I don't have much. Duarte *père* was a dealer for years out on the West Coast. He was a Vineyard boy who left young and made good. His son preferred this coast and lived here while he worked with his father. They both had good eyes for art and did well. The buzz is that they were like most people: honest for the most part, but willing to stretch a point here and there. Maybe more willing than most. Business being business, you understand."

I did. I had done some stretching myself upon occasion. "I owe you a six-pack," I said.

"Make it Ipswich Ale. Say, is something the matter with you? You don't sound quite normal."

"I'm okay. You'll get your beer of choice. One last thing. Did you ever meet any of these people in your travels?"

"No. Why?"

"I thought that if you had, you might have some private impressions."

"Sorry. No private impressions. I do have one suggestion, though. Keeping in mind that the possession or promise of big money can lead people to do things they might not otherwise do, I'd be careful if I were you."

Yes. I'd been lucky and now I'd be careful. "Mahsimba gave me the same advice," I said. "Thanks."

Life doesn't stop or step aside just because we have narrow escapes. My family had to eat, for instance, so I thawed out the bluefish fillets and began putting supper together while I thought about the gunshot and the job I'd taken on. My moving hands actually began to soothe me, and allowed me to come back closer to an even keel.

I didn't know who the shooter was, but I knew I was dealing with at least one or two liars, and probably more, and that made things more complicated than I'd have preferred them to be. But on the other hand, I expected people to lie when they thought it was in their best interests to do so, so I wasn't offended.

By the time the kids got home from school, I was feeling more angry than frightened, and I took that to be a good thing. I fed the tots snacks and spent some time with them in the tree house, where, by hunching down and pulling my knees up under my chin, I could sit in their main living area, between the two spreading branches that held their respective private rooms.

I'd always admired Tarzan's tree house in the old Johnny Weissmuller movies, and was pleased to have one for my children. It lacked Jane and Cheeta, of course, but it had a ladder leading up from the ground and a rope you could use to swing back down, so it wasn't bad.

I was always worried about one of the kids falling out and getting seriously hurt, but I kept that feeling to myself just as my father had done when my sister and I had had our tree house when we were little. Biting back fear is one price of parenthood.

About the time Zee was due home, I swung down to the ground and got back to work in the kitchen.

But instead of the sound of her Jeep coming down the driveway, I got a telephone call.

"Hi," she said. "I'm over at Mattie's house having a cup of tea. I'll be home in an hour or so."

"Supper will be waiting," I said. "See you then. Best to Mattie and all."

"I'll convey your solicitations."

The phone clicked and I looked at it for a moment before hanging up. I remembered what Mattie had said to me earlier in the day and thought she was probably right. I felt curiously devoid of emotions about Zee and Mahsimba and wondered if I was denying something I should be letting come up out of my subconscious so I could deal with it. In any case, I didn't plan to tell Zee about the gunshot. She already had enough on her plate.

I set the table and checked to make sure that Diana and Joshua were still alive. They were.

Oliver Underfoot and Velcro came in through their cat door, and Oliver wound himself around my legs before joining Velcro at the cat dish.

A half hour before supper, I called the children inside and had them wash up before eating.

"Pa?"

"What?"

"Can we have a—"

"No."

Something in my voice kept Joshua from finishing his sentence. He turned away.

"I'm sorry for interrupting you," I said. "Can you have a what?"

"A dog."

"No. No dogs." My refusal sounded no different from other refusals I'd tendered in the past, but I realized that I'd almost said yes, because of nerves or out of guilt for being sharp with my son. I'd have to be careful or I'd have a dog underfoot in spite of myself. Guilt was no doubt responsible for many a household pet.

Zee's Jeep came down the driveway right on schedule, and I was setting the food on the table as she came through the door. Her face was aglow from within.

"Sorry to be late," she said. She'd loosed her hair from the bun she wore at work, and her long tresses fell over her shoulders, shining darkly as a night sky.

"Your timing is perfect," I said. "Red wine or white? We're having stuffed bluefish."

"White, then." She took her seat and smiled at her children. "What have you two been up to? How was school?"

The three of them ate as she listened to the reports of their day that I'd heard earlier.

"How's Mattie?" I asked after a while.

Zee smiled a smile that looked almost unstrained. "Fine. She and John are still busy getting straightened away for the summer, and the twins are busy with their horses."

No mention of Mahsimba.

"Is John still working on *Gawain*?"

"I believe he's still at it," said Zee.

"His computer must be a big help to him."

She touched her napkin to her lips. "I imagine it is. They say you can find any information you want on the Internet."

"I'm going out for a while after supper," I said. "I shouldn't be too long."

"Where are you going? What are you going to do?"

"I'm going to try for some blues at Metcalf's Hole. I thought you might want to be with the kids for a couple of hours."

There was an awkward moment of silence. Then Diana said, "You can help me read, Ma. I'd like that!"

"Me, too, Ma," exclaimed her son, not to be outdone.

Zee stared at me, then smiled at her children. "I'll help both of you. Now, finish your plates so you can have dessert. I think there's ice cream in the freezer."

After the dishes were washed and stacked to dry, I put my rod on the roof rack of the Land Cruiser. The summer night was falling slowly. Zee stood in the lighted doorway. I blew her a kiss and drove away. But I didn't go to South Beach; I went to West Tisbury, to Matthew Duarte's place. I wasn't going to let being shot at change my plans, but my eyes were looking in every direction as I drove.

21

The slanting summer light lasted late into the evening and made my job difficult, since it was more likely that people might see sneaky me, but I was undeterred.

Not too far beyond Matthew Duarte's property I checked one last time to see if anyone was following me, then pulled off the highway and into the yard of the house where Zee had lived before we married. The place was almost exactly on the West Tisbury–Chilmark line, and I'd never been sure which town the building was really in. The house was small and neat and not yet occupied by summer people, and it was hidden by trees from the road. Not too many years earlier, I'd spent a goodly amount of time in that house before I'd persuaded Zee to live with me in mine. Now I parked the Land Cruiser under a tall oak, got my flashlight, my picks, and a pair of thin rubber gloves, and walked out past the house into the field behind it.

A hundred years before, the island had not been the tourist destination it now was. True, Oak Bluffs had long been a popular place for camp meetings and associated summer socializing, but the greater part of the island had been devoted to farming and raising sheep, and was devoid of the trees and underbrush that now covered so much of it. The small field behind the house was all that remained of once wide-open grazing lands divided by stone walls.

To the east, through second- and third-growth trees, I could see Matthew Duarte's home and barn. I walked that way, moving slowly, with many pauses to look for other people and to make sure I wasn't seen from the road.

Long before, I'd once walked with equal care through a faraway forest, led by Sergeant Joe Begay on my first and last patrol in a war-torn land. My caution had done me no good at all on that occasion, for we'd been spotted by an efficient enemy mortar man or cannoneer (I've never been sure which) who dropped shell after shell upon us before he and his weapon were finally silenced and those of us who survived his assault had been taken out by helicopter. I still had occasional nightmares about that attack and would wake up sweating and full of fear, my ears ringing from the memory of the incredible noise of bombardment.

It took me half an hour to get to Duarte's yard. There I lay behind some tufts of tall grass and surveyed the place for activity. There was none: no people, no cars, no movement. Around me the darkness became thicker. I waited until it was thicker still, then got to my feet and circumnavigated Duarte's barn.

Aside from the front door to the office, there were large, sliding barn doors in the front and back of the building and windows on all sides. All the doors were locked and all but the office windows were barred and boarded.

I then eased around the house, just to be sure, but

saw no sign of anyone being there. Sam Hopewell had apparently gone home for the night and left no watchman. I dug my lock picks out of my pocket and went to the office door in the front of the barn.

I'd gotten the picks years before at a yard sale given by a woman who was getting rid of her dead husband's things. She hadn't even known what they were, and I'd wondered at the time if her deceased hubby had had a secret life she'd known nothing of. As for me, I was more overt about my interest in the picks, and kept them, along with various locks, on the coffee table in our living room so I could practice their arcane usage when relaxing in the evening. They were taboo to my children and a joke to Zee and our occasional guests. I wondered if Zee would notice that the picks were gone this evening.

If opening the outer office door triggered an alarm in the police station, I was in instant trouble, but I'd seen no sign of such wiring during my entrances and exits from the office and felt fairly sure that the building's real security began inside.

I am not the world's champion lock picker, but the lock on the door was a simple one and I was quickly inside. I shut the door, flipped on the flashlight, and followed its beam down the hall to the inner office door, where another common lock was no more of a problem than the first.

Inside the office, I put on the gloves. I hadn't needed them earlier because I'd quite publicly visited the office before and had certainly left my finger-prints on both doors. Now, however, I would be putting my hands where they had no business being. I pulled the blinds on the windows and went to the

desk once used by Matthew Duarte. There I found
the wires leading under the Oriental rug to the
inner wall. They ran up one leg of the desk and
disappeared.

I looked under the center drawer but saw nothing. Duarte apparently had his alarm switch inside a
drawer. But which one? And was that drawer itself
wired to some sort of alarm set to go off if some
secret act did not precede its opening? I didn't know
enough about Duarte to guess his degree of caution.

I tested a side drawer. Locked. I put the beam of
the flashlight on it and saw no keyhole. I looked at
other drawers. Only the center drawer had a keyhole. Duarte's desk was one of those that had side
drawers that unlocked only when the center drawer
was opened. I picked the center drawer lock and slid
the drawer open.

If I had been Duarte, where would I have put the
switch to arm or disarm my alarm system?

Some place not too obvious but easy to get to. I
slid the drawer out very slowly, looking for a switch.
No switch. I tried another drawer. Nothing. The
switch was two drawers down on the right side. I
flicked it off.

No sirens, no noise of any kind. I went to the
front of the barn and opened the door a crack. I listened for a police siren or the sound of a car coming
into the driveway. Nothing. But I was nervous, so I
went outside, shutting the door behind me, and
crossed to the dark shadows under a grove of oaks
on the far side of the yard. I stayed there for many
minutes, listening.

No police cars came.

I went back to the barn and let myself inside,

locking the outer door behind me. The door in the side of the hallway had a much better lock than the ones I'd encountered earlier, and I had to work quite a while to get it open. When at last it swung into the room it guarded, my fingers were shaking. I apparently lacked the necessary nerve to be successful in the breaking-and-entering profession.

There was a light switch beside the door, but for the moment I ignored it in favor of my flashlight. I was in a large, cool room, with windows that were not only covered with plywood but heavily curtained as well. At one end of the room was a small, enclosed wood-shop area where, I guessed, Duarte had made packing crates when he needed them. Through the large windows that separated that room from this one I could see plywood stacked against a wall, several power saws, and a workbench. In the wall across from the door where I stood there were double doors barred by a steel rod.

I was in a climate-controlled storage area. Paintings, sculpture, ceramics, wood carvings, furniture, antique lamps, rugs, and other items filled shelves and storage bins. Boxes and crates were neatly stacked against one wall, and there was a large, old-fashioned safe beside a curtained and boarded window.

Although no judge of art, I recognized pieces from the Orient, others from Africa, Europe, Central or South America, and still others from the American Southwest. When I decided that it was safe to turn on the overhead lights and take a better look, I saw something that I'd missed: a desk and chair tucked against the wall next to the barred double doors. I shut the door behind me and went to them, flicked on a reading light above the desk, and sat down in the swivel chair. The desk was locked. Matthew had been a locker.

Some people are that way; they lock everything: their houses, their cars, their desks, everything they own that can be locked. They apparently believe they're surrounded by thieves. I only lock my car when I go to Boston. The rest of the time everything I own, with the exception of our gun locker at home, I leave unlocked. And even the gun locker has its key lying on its top so I'll know where to find it. Locks, as someone observed and as I now proved with my picks, are only good for keeping honest people out.

The contents of Matthew's desk were fairly sparse, and I guessed that he used this desk much less than his big one in the office. Its drawers held only a few recent papers: bills, paid and unpaid, records of transactions, invoices, and the other printed matter that computers promised but have failed to replace. Probably, I thought, he used the desk as a convenience when accepting or shipping merchandise, then later transferred the records to his and Hopewell's desks in the office.

I turned off the lights, unbarred the double doors, and followed the beam of my flashlight out onto a low loading platform. There was enough space between the platform and the far wall of the barn for a large truck to pull in through the double doors in one end of the building, load or unload, and exit through the doors at the opposite end.

There was no starlight seeping in around the edges of the doors, and the windows here were also curtained as well as boarded. Duarte had been secretive, indeed. I found a switch and turned on the lights.

Above the acclimatized storage room was the loft of the barn. In the dust in front of the platform were truck tracks. Big ones and small ones. On the platform there were dollies leaning against the wall and a small forklift parked beside a ramp leading to the ground. Nothing looked unusual. It was a commonplace loading platform, such as you see behind or beside many a business, where Matthew Duarte received and sent the goods that were his livelihood.

I walked to the end of the platform and saw that there was a portable generator at the far end of the area. Emergency power for the climate-controlled room, in case normal power failed, which it does with some regularity when storms blow over Martha's Vineyard.

Beyond the generator was a tack room, filled with the sweet, horse smell of leather and oils. The Skye twins would have approved.

I went back into the storage room and studied the safe. It was very old and very heavy, an antique in its own right, but powerfully constructed. Quite beyond my powers as a picker.

Still, even people who go to great lengths to have yegg-proof safes almost always keep their lock combinations written down somewhere, in case of emergencies. It is another example of the paradoxical human character that the combinations are often kept close to the safes themselves.

I tried the back of the safe, then the top, but no combination revealed itself to me. I looked around the room. The most permanent and convenient piece of furniture in sight was the desk by the door. Could it be . . . ?

I found the combination on the back of the smallest drawer in the desk. Ah, the world of crime lost a real slicker when I opted for the honest life.

The great safe opened on oiled hinges.

Inside were coins and jewels and small items of art deemed, perhaps, too easy to misplace or too valuable to be stored elsewhere. There was also a good amount of cash, and I withstood the temptation to take it although I could really think of no good reason not to. I was apparently one of those people whose upbringing didn't prevent them from having sinful thoughts but did prevent them from enjoying them.

I slid open a drawer and found a ledger.

Hmmmm. What was it about this book that Matthew had valued enough to keep it secreted here? I opened it and found myself looking at ordinary-appearing records, notations, and figures.

As near as I could tell as I leafed through the pages, Matthew had done business with Gerald Jenkins, Georgie Hall, Charles Mauch, and many other people I'd never heard of except in the local papers, where I'd read about their social, political, and humanitarian activities. If I was interpreting the sales figures correctly, all of Matthew's clients had more money than I did. There were off-island customers as well as islanders, but the Vineyard buyers were apparently his principal clients.

I found the record of the sale of the Bakuba sculpture to Georgie Hall, and noted that unless you knew that Gerald Jenkins had been slickered by Duarte, you'd never guess it by reading this file.

I found papers recording payments to UPS, FedEx, and local movers and truckers, including several to Periera Food Service. Matthew had appar-

ently been yet another islander willing to pay Miguel
to do mainland shopping for him.

Further along in the book I came to writings that
were too much for me to grasp, made up as they were
of cryptic notations and figures, and names of people
and objects that seemed in code but perhaps were just
the lingo of men in his trade. I wondered if it was this
seemingly ciphered writing that Matthew had wished
to keep locked away, and if Sam Hopewell knew
about this ledger. Were these arcane words the
records of Matthew's less-than-legal dealings?

If I'd been the hero in a spy movie, I'd no doubt
have known the answers to those questions as well as
which pages to photograph with my minicamera,
had I owned one, but, alas, I was as untrained in
espionage as I was in bookkeeping, so I put things
back where I found them and shut the safe's door. In
time some agent more legitimate than I would come
seeking its contents.

I looked at my watch. I'd been there for some time.
Maybe too long. I turned off the lights and went back
through the storage room to the hall, again following
the beam of my flashlight. As I opened the outside
door of the hallway, I heard the sound of a car engine
and saw headlights sweep into the driveway. I pulled
the door almost shut, then froze as the car came into
the yard. The police.

22

I was trapped, but Fate, ever fickle, chose to aid me. The police officer turned his cruiser in a slow circle, sweeping headlights across the front of the barn, then parked facing the house. The second the lights passed the door I nipped outside, pushed the door closed behind me, and ran across the dark yard into the greater darkness beneath the oak trees, reaching them just as the car came to a halt, its headlights on the door of the house, and the driver's door opened.

I stopped running and lay gently down in the high grass. The sounds of my beating heart and of the grass bending and breaking beneath my body seemed so loud that they must surely be heard across the yard, I thought, and my efforts to slow my gasps for breath seemed futile.

But the young police officer paid no attention to me or my many noises. With his long flashlight in his hand, he moved leisurely to the door of the house, rattled the knob, then moved on around a corner and disappeared. In the lights from the cruiser I recognized the young West Tisbury cop I'd twice seen since finding Duarte's body. The beam of his flashlight shone briefly on some bushes as he circled the house, checking windows.

I didn't wait for him to reappear, but got to my feet

and walked carefully west until I was beyond the oaks that encircled the yard. There, from the security of a distant tree trunk, I turned back and watched the young officer reappear in the yard. He went to the office door in the front of the barn and gave it a shake, and I was glad I'd made sure that the door had locked itself behind me. He checked the double doors, then went out of sight around the barn, his light dancing on surrounding undergrowth as he went.

Hopewell or Connie Duarte had apparently requested and gotten security checks from West Tisbury's finest. I waited no longer but went away across the fields and under the trees until I got back to the Land Cruiser. As I drove back to Edgartown I realized that I'd been sweating. At the head of my driveway I told myself that nobody would be there waiting for me. No one was.

Zee was in the oversized T-shirt she sometimes wore as a nightgown. There was a picture of a tiger on it and the words "Queen of the Jungle." Usually we both slept naked. She was headed for bed. Her dark hair and eyes and her sleek body made me think, not for the first time, of a black panther.

"Any luck?" she asked.

"I never saw a swirl."

"Oh, well. You can always go to the A and P. They have a fish department."

"Ha, ha. Very amusing." It was a familiar local jest among fishermen. Actually, I sometimes did buy fish from the A & P, but never anything that swam in Vineyard waters.

Zee went into the bedroom and I put my lock picks back on the coffee table. When I got into bed a bit later, Zee seemed asleep. I lay down and put my hand on her hip. She didn't move. I slid the hand down her smooth thigh. She still didn't move. After a while I took the hand away and turned on my reading light. The summer night was warm, and I read many chapters before I was able to sleep.

The next morning was Saturday, and I remembered little of what I'd read. Whatever had been between my mind and my book was still there. I had a slight headache.

At breakfast Zee said, "You've been working hard. I think you need a break. It's a lovely day. Let's take Mahsimba to Wasque. They don't have an ocean in Zimbabwe, so he should have a beach day while he's on the island." She paused, then added, "Maybe John and Mattie would like to come, too."

I chewed and swallowed my mouthful of bagel, cream cheese, red onion, and smoked bluefish. Normally delish but today tasteless. "You can but ask," I said.

"I will. It'll be fun." She went into the kitchen to the phone.

When the dishes were washed and stacked, I put the rods on the roof rack of the Land Cruiser and ice in the fish box in the back along with the beach umbrella and the canvas bag of other essentials: the bedspread we used as a beach blanket, towels, a Frisbee, and plastic shovels and buckets in case we were overcome by an irresistible urge to build a sand castle.

When I went back inside, Zee was making sandwiches and packing the cooler. There was a radiance about her that held me in thrall. I wished I were its cause, but knew I was not.

"Pa?"

"What?"

"Are we going fishing?"

"We're going to the beach. We'll fish if there are any fish, and maybe even if there aren't."

"Good. Do you have our rods?"

"Yes." Their little rods were in the rack. If there were fish close in, near the surf, they might be able to reach them with their short casts. You're never too young to start trying for blues.

Zee put the lid on the cooler. "Beer, soft drinks, sandwiches, pickles, potato chips, and pretzels. Everything we need." She seemed happy. "John and Mattie and Mahsimba will meet us at Wasque. If we leave now, we should get there for the last two hours of the east tide."

Around Martha's Vineyard the tides rise to the east and fall to the west. At Wasque Point the fishing is good two hours before the change.

I got into my swimsuit and pulled on a pair of shorts over it, then put on a T-shirt I'd gotten in the thrift shop where I get most of my clothes.

Zee and the kids were also garbed for the beach, the June sun was rising higher into a powder-blue sky, and there was no reason to linger, so we didn't.

We drove through Edgartown and went on to Katama. There, early-rising June people, intent upon getting in a full day of their expensive island vacations, were already gathering on the beach, putting up their umbrellas, spreading their blankets, and testing the water with their toes. We didn't join them, but instead got into four-wheel drive, took a left, and drove over the sand to Chappaquiddick.

To our left, beyond the waters of Katama Bay, we

could see the white buildings of Edgartown; to our right, a mile or so offshore, there was a fishing boat, its spreaders making it look like a giant insect walking over the water.

We saw gulls, terns, plovers, oyster catchers, and an osprey before we got to Chappy. We also salvaged a float that had washed up onto the beach and thus were guaranteed, before we even wet a line, that we'd not go home empty-handed; the float would join the dozens of others we'd found on the beach over the years and which now adorned the walls of the shed out in back of our house and gave the place a perhaps excessively Vineyardish cachet.

We fetched the Dyke Bridge and followed East Beach south toward Wasque. On the horizon we could see the faint irregularity that was the island of Muskeget, the westernmost part of Nantucket. Farther north, across the sound, was the misty outline of Cape Cod's south shore, running east toward Chatham. There were Jeeps scattered along the beach, surrounded by chairs and beach blankets and fronted by fishermen and -women making casts out into the water. Over the earth and sea the sky arched blue and cloudless beneath the summer sun.

The beach at Wasque Point grows and shrinks according to the whims of the wind and sea. That year it was wide and long. The rip was arching out from the line of surf and there were Jeeps ahead of us with bluefish lying under them out of the sun. The rods of the fishermen were bending with a happy regularity.

I found a spot to park and Zee was out of the truck in a flash.

"Come on!" she cried.

She snagged her rod from the roof rack, trotted down to the surf, and made her cast. Her green Roberts arched far out and splashed on the edge of the rip. A moment later I saw the white swirl of a striking fish and the bend of her rod. She looked back, laughing, then turned and began to reel.

A thing of beauty is a joy forever. I leaned on the steering wheel and watched her bring the fish in.

"Come on, Pa! Help us get our rods!"

Joshua and Diana were too short to reach the roof rack. I got out and took down their rods, and they ran down to the water.

Their casts were straight but far too short; however, they kept at it while Zee landed her fish and brought it up to the truck, grinning. A nice five-pounder, flopping and twisting.

"Get down there!" she said. "You won't catch them with your rod on the rack!"

I took her fish by the gills and removed the hook from its mouth. "I'll be right there. Catch another one." I picked up the fish knife and cut the fish's throat and tossed it under the truck. Zee gave me an odd look and went back to the water.

I went down to where the kids were casting and reeling. "I think they're out too far for you," I said. "If you want, I'll see if I can get your lure out farther. Then you can reel in."

"Here," said Diana, while Joshua gave my offer thought.

Her rig was so small and light that I couldn't get much length to the cast, but I put it out a little farther than she could, and gave the rod back to her. "Be patient," I said. "There have been days when everybody around me was catching fish and I couldn't catch a cold. When you get your line in, I'll cast it again."

"Okay, Pa."

Zee was on again. I could hear the line sing as her rod bent. The water had become alive with fish, and rods were bent as far as I could see down the beach.

Joshua allowed me to cast his plug. I did better with his gear than I had with his sister's, but I still didn't get the lure out where the fish were. "Keep at it," I told him. "Sometimes the school gets closer to shore. If that happens, you should be in the middle of them."

The children reeled and I cast their lines. Zee made those long, lovely casts of hers and soon had a half dozen fish under the truck. Finally she put her rod in one of the spikes on our front bumper, got my rod off the roof, and brought it down to me.

"Here. You fish for a while and I'll cast for the sprats. I think they're moving in; I got that last one about half a cast out."

"Okay."

I loosed the redheaded Roberts from the guide, walked a few steps away, and made my cast. The lure splashed and I reeled it in. There was a swirl of white, but the fish missed. I slowed my reeling. Another swirl and this time I felt the brief touch of a fish that had almost but not quite made a solid hit. I reeled in and made another cast. More swirls as the voracious blues snapped at my lure but passed without taking it.

On the third cast one got his teeth around it, and I set the hooks and pulled him in, lifting the tip of the rod high, then reeling down as he fought to stay free, twisting and leaping and racing away, but was brought slowly, fatally, to the shore. I timed the surf to let the last wave help me sweep him up onto the sand, then got a hand in his gills and carried him, flopping and jerking, up to the truck. A fighter to the very last. I got the lure out of his mouth and cut his throat.

"Very nice," said a voice I recognized.

John Skye's Jeep had pulled in beside ours, and he, Mattie, and Mahsimba were busy unloading beach gear. I hooked my lure in a guide and set my rod in a spike beside Zee's.

"Where are the twins?" I asked. "I thought they'd jump at the chance to brown the meat on a day like this."

"The girls, I'm happy to say, are gainfully employed this summer, working as waitresses in some of the island's favorite watering holes. Both are on noon shifts today, so only the old folks get to play."

Mattie gave me a kiss and Mahsimba shook my hand and peered under the truck.

"You have caught some nice fish."

"All but this last one are Zee's," I said.

"Ah. I should have guessed that she is an excellent fisherman. Oh, look at your son!"

I turned toward the water and I saw that Joshua's rod was bent almost double. He was on!

"He has himself a very nice fish," said Mahsimba as Joshua was yanked toward the surf and staggered back again.

"Perhaps he can use some assistance."

Zee was watching Joshua closely but keeping her hands away from his rod. I could see her lips moving as she advised and encouraged him. "He has all the help he needs," I said.

Mahsimba nodded, and we watched the drama unfold before us, with Joshua hauling back and trying to reel down before his fish threw the lure. Slowly he began to gain line, and on both sides of him other fishermen reeled in and stood watching him. I remembered catching my own first good-sized fish, and was filled with a wild joy as Joshua backed away from the water, hauling the fish closer and closer to shore. Then the fish was racing back and forth in the surf and I held my breath, for many a fish has been lost right there in the last inch of water.

But this one wasn't lost. Flipping and thrashing, he came slithering out of the last wave and up onto the shining sand, and Zee was on him in a flash, making sure he stayed caught. She put a bare foot on his side, grabbed him by the gills, and carried him up onto the dry sand, where her exhausted son stood panting and beaming, so tired that he was shaking. She put her arm around her boy's shoulders and, laughing and brilliant-eyed, brought him and his fish up to the truck as the other fishermen, smiling, turned back to the sea and made their casts.

"Pa! Pa! Joshua's fish is huge!" Diana's voice was full of joy and wonder as she came running up from the water, carrying her own little rod.

Huge enough. I weighed the fish out at seven and a half pounds.

"Well done," I said to Joshua.

"I thought he was going to pull me in," said Joshua. "I didn't think I could hold on any longer."

"You did just fine. I'm proud of you. We'll have this guy for supper, if that's all right with you. Stuffed bluefish again."

He nodded happily, still panting.

"You'd better get some rest," I said. "Your fishing muscles are probably pretty tired."

"Okay, Pa. Can I have a soda? I need a drink."

"You bet. You know where the cooler is. Help yourself."

"Me, too, Pa?"

"Sure, Diana."

The children put their rods in spikes and headed for the beach blanket and the cooler.

I turned and saw Mahsimba, John, Mattie, and Zee talking and laughing as they looked at Joshua's fish under the truck.

I opened the back of the Land Cruiser, then, two by two, surf-rinsed sand from our blues and put them in the box on top of the crushed ice. We had plenty of fish.

I walked over to the grown-ups.

"You should be proud of your son," said Mahsimba, smiling. "He fought a mighty battle."

"I am proud of him," I said. "Are you a fisherman yourself?"

"I am," he said.

"Zimbabwe is famous for its fishing," said John. "Trout in the mountains and tiger fish in Lake Kariba."

"But no surf casting as you do here," said Mahsimba. "We fly-fish for trout and use boats for tiger fish, which, if one may boast, fight as fiercely as your bluefish and have as many teeth." He held out a hand and I saw a thin scar along one finger. "A memorial to a careless moment removing a hook. I'm fortunate to have my finger at all. Tiger fish are related to piranhas."

"Let's take a walk up the beach," I said. "You can

see how different people make their casts. If you look closely, you'll see a few scarred fingers among the locals, too."

"I would enjoy a walk," said Mahsimba.

"And while you two are gone," said Mattie, taking my wife's arm, "Zee will bring us up-to-date on all the latest gossip. People in the ER know all the juicy stuff!"

"We'll be back in time for the first beer of the morning," I said.

Zee hesitated, then looked quickly at Mattie as Mahsimba and I turned and walked away.

23

"Your island is lovely and varied. This spot is very different from the villages I've seen."

Mahsimba was strolling barefoot beside me, carrying his shoes in one hand. His shirt and shorts were neat and pressed, unlike mine.

We looked at the line of fishermen as we passed behind their trucks going westward toward the wooden walkway and stairs that led to the parking lot on the top of the bluffs overlooking the Swan Pond. Different fishermen used different motions when they cast and when they reeled in. Some, like me, brought their rods straight back before casting; others threw sidearm. Some used every muscle in their backs and arms; others made seemingly effortless flips. Some reeled with their rod tips high; others kept their tips close to the water. Some reeled hard and fast; others reeled slowly, gently. All of them were catching fish.

"Is it possible that there are fish here like this every day?" asked Mahsimba.

"No. This is a blitz. The fish may be gone any moment, or they may stay here for hours. Some days you can cast here from dawn to dusk and never see a fish."

"In Africa it's the same. There are always fish and

there are always fishermen, but the two are not necessarily in the same place at the same time."

A universal truth, no doubt.

We ducked under the rope barrier that prevented Jeeps from going farther west, crossed the board walkway, and went on, leaving the trucks and the fishermen behind us.

"You wish to speak with me, J.W."

"Yes."

"About your wife, perhaps?"

I looked into those unfathomable golden eyes. "No, not about her."

He arched a brow. "What, then?"

"About you and David Brownington."

"Ah. What would you like to know?"

"The truth."

He cocked his head slightly. "And what truth is that?"

"The one about the relationship between you and Brownington. The one about the people you really work for."

We walked on. To our left the dancing waves of the Wasque rip curved out to sea. On the far horizon by Porky's Island the surf was white.

"Tell me your thoughts," said Mahsimba.

"My thoughts are that you work or at least worked at one time for the UN and maybe for Interpol and that your onetime friend David Brownington once did the same before creating a consulting firm and hiring out his skills to the other side. My thoughts are that right now, you may be working for yourself, not for the UN or Interpol or the Zimbabwe government. My thoughts are that you may not have actually lied about who you are and what you're doing, but that you deceived me and John Skye and Stan Crandel from the beginning. My thoughts are that I don't like being lied to by the people I work with."

We walked on. "I see," said Mahsimba. "You have resources I had not anticipated, J.W." He gave me his smile. "I apologize for underestimating your capacities."

"But not for deceiving me."

"I regret that I did so. Deception is a tool of my work, I fear, but in this case its use was clearly an error."

"But only because you were found out."

"Indeed, that is so. It has been my experience that most people are more trusting and speak more freely if one is understood to be an employee of a museum or an agent for a law enforcement agency rather than if one is an independent contractor working for a private organization. There are exceptions, of course, of which you are perhaps one."

Everybody lies at one time or another. Amateurs do it to deceive themselves and others who affect their everyday lives; professionals do it for business reasons.

At the west end of Swan Pond we turned and walked back.

"I have to know what's going on," I said. "I don't want to walk into trouble that I can't anticipate."

"Does this mean that you might continue working with me?" Mahsimba's voice held a note of mild surprise.

"Maybe. Are you really an independent contractor, or do you still have links to Interpol and the UN?"

"I have been granted leave from my official duties with Interpol, and have taken temporary employment with a private firm which, in turn, has been hired by the government of Zimbabwe."

"To find the eagles."

"Yes. And to return them to my country."

"Tell me about Brownington Limited."

Mahsimba gave himself some time to consider his reply. Then he said, "David was and perhaps still is my friend, so his new life is of more than just professional interest to me; it's personal. The organization that has employed him also wants the eagles. So far, David has been one step ahead of me in the search, so he found Matthew Duarte before I did."

"Which may have been a fatal mistake. How do you know so much about Brownington's activities if the two of you aren't on the same side?"

He held an imaginary cell phone to his ear. "Modern technology not only allows people to communicate rapidly over great distances, but also allows others to sometimes intercept those communications. Both the lawful and the lawless have those capacities."

"What makes the people who hired Brownington so anxious to get their hands on the eagles?"

Mahsimba smiled. "A curious combination of greed and sentimentality. After the mercenary, Parsons, stole the eagles from Crompton, the white farmer whose family had owned them for so long, Crompton soon found himself without a farm, too. His land was taken by the successful revolutionaries.

"Being a resourceful businessman with a knowledge of African art, Crompton went into the import-export business, specializing in the international sale of art objects. In the last thirty-five years he has built a very successful organization. Much of his trade, need I say, is in illegal objects, and Interpol is doing its best to put him in jail."

"So far in vain, I take it."

"So far. But even while Crompton has been thriving economically, he has never forgotten the eagles. He thinks they are rightfully his, and he wants them back. His feelings were very hurt when Parsons stole them, and when he could afford to do so, he began to look for Parsons. He hired David Brownington and David found him. You know the rest.

"I've been told by Sergeant Agganis, to whom I showed my identity card as a member of Interpol, that blood samples from members of Brownington's family have arrived in Boston and that DNA tests will soon determine whether your Headless Horseman is indeed my friend David."

"I take it that Interpol and the organization you now represent have the same interests in the eagles."

"Indeed. Interpol works closely with governments to curtail international crime, including trade in stolen artifacts. The interests of the organization by whom I'm currently employed are those of Zimbabwe, which believes the eagles are its property and wants them back."

"And your interests are purely economical?"

"It's true that I'm making more money at the moment than when I am on salary for Interpol, but I'm also a Zimbabwean and have a personal interest in having the birds returned to their homeland.

"My supervisor at Interpol, who is always complaining about a shortage of money, is pleased to have me on this temporary private assignment because the costs of my search are being borne by my employers."

Head cops are always complaining about their departments being short of money.

"A tangled web," I said.

"Yes."

"Can you give me any reason to believe anything you've just told me?"

"I cannot. Eventually the truth will be clear to anyone interested, but until then you must trust your instincts."

We came to the line of trucks and I saw that only about half of the fishermen were still casting. The others had their rods in spikes and were gathered in clusters, talking.

"The blitz has passed," I said.

"Sic transit gloria mundi."

Ahead of us were our own Jeeps. My children were in their swimsuits and Zee had doffed her shirt and shorts and was wearing her black bikini.

"Your wife is an extraordinarily beautiful woman," said Mahsimba.

"Yes."

"Fairer than the evening air clad in the beauty of a thousand stars."

"But the devil will come and Faustus must be damned. Several months ago she shot a man to death and maimed another. They were attacking her and our daughter. She hasn't been quite the same since. When you get closer you'll be able to see the scar of the bullet fired by the man she killed."

"My God!"

"I owe her most of the joy in my life. I'll never step between her and happiness of her own, but if anyone hurts her, they'll have me to deal with."

"I understand."

"There's something else you should know," I said. "But I don't want Zee to know because she has enough on her mind already. Yesterday somebody took a shot at me. Apparently my snooping around has spooked somebody. You're snooping, too, so be careful." I told him what had happened.

He took a few steps, then stopped us both. "I think it's best if I fire you right now, J.W. I thank you for all you've done, but I don't want your blood on my hands."

"I don't think I want to stop," I said. "If you want to fire me, that's fine, but I plan to keep going."

He studied me, then nodded. "I believe I would do the same. But we must both be careful."

We walked on until we came up to the Jeeps.

"The fish are gone and the food is ready," said Mattie. "It's time to eat."

So we did that, sitting on beach blankets, drinking beer and sodas with our sandwiches.

"I'm sorry you didn't get a chance to fish," said Zee, who was sitting beside Mahsimba.

"The fish will be back," said Mahsimba, smiling that smile. "If they come soon, I'll be waiting for them."

"Spoken like a Red Sox fan," said John. "Wait until next year."

"I do not know these red socks," said Mahsimba.

"Explaining the Boston Red Sox may take some time," said John. "The Red Sox are Boston's professional baseball team. Do you know baseball?"

"I've heard of it. Rather like cricket, I'm told."

"There are similarities, but one big difference between other professional sports teams and the Red Sox is that the Sox never, ever win the championship. Thus the famous phrase, 'Wait until next year.' It represents the eternal triumph of hope over experience."

Zee was a Sox fan, and had strong opinions about the team.

"D," she now said. "Never enough D or pitching. Sluggers, usually, but mostly not much in the way of fielding or pitchers. There's Nomar and Pedro and Manny, of course, but not much else. I blame management."

"Take it easy," I said. "You may dislocate an arm, waving it like that."

She ignored me. "They know they can fill Fenway with any kind of team at all, so they won't shell out enough money to buy themselves a winner. Boston hasn't won a Series since 1918, for God's sake! Look at the Yankees! They win about every other Series that's played. And why? Because they'll pay their players and they've got smart management! If you decide to live in America, Mahsimba, save yourself a lot of grief and root for the Yankees!"

"Sacrilege," said John mildly. "I'm shocked, Zeolinda, shocked to hear such words fall from your lips."

She grinned and raised both hands in surrender. "You're right, John. I'm just being bitter. Anybody at all can root for a winner like the Yankees, Mahsimba, but you have to have character to be a Red Sox fan."

I saw Mahsimba's eyes touch the bullet scar across her ribs beneath her left arm before he laughed and let his gaze float to Mattie, who was saying little but seeing much.

"What do you think, Mattie?" he asked. "Should I

become a fan of your Red Sox or of the famous New York Yankees, who are known even in my country?"

"All the people on these blankets are Red Sox fans, for better or for worse," said Mattie, looking back and forth between him and Zee. "But you get to choose."

— 24 —

The next morning I left Zee and the children at home and drove to Vineyard Haven, where I knew a guy who worked for the Steamship Authority. He owed me a favor and got a kick out of snooping and telling tales, a nice combination as long as you never told him anything you didn't want made public knowledge.

"Jim," I said, "I'd like to know how often the Periera Food Service truck goes back and forth to the mainland."

"Why do you want to know?"

"So I can free you from the favor you owe me and lift that burden from your soul."

"I mean really."

"So do I."

He sighed and turned to his computer. After a lot of that keyboard tapping that computer people do, some muttering, and a few crude words, he turned to me.

"Steady as clockwork," he said. "He takes the seven A.M. boat over and comes back on the eight-fifteen P.M. on Tuesdays, Thursdays, and Saturdays during the summer and on Wednesdays during the winter. Done that for three years and has reservations for the next six months. I guess he does a good business for three months and less for the other nine, like everybody else on this island. And why not? Who wants to pay Vineyard prices?"

Not me, for sure. "Thanks," I said. "We're all even, Jim. You can sleep with an innocent heart."

"You're a trip, J.W. You know, if you'd just break down and get yourself a computer of your own, you could probably save your friends a lot of work."

"No computers for me," I said. "I have problems with any gadgets more complicated than a straight-blade knife."

"I suppose I'll be wasting my time reminding you that this is the twenty-first century, not the nineteenth."

I went out without answering.

The last time I'd seen Miguel Periera had been on Thursday at Georgie Hall's house. She'd given him a shopping list that apparently he'd planned to fill when he went to America the next day.

I drove to Oak Bluffs and stopped at the state police office on Temahigan Avenue. Years before, the building had been painted an odd shade of blue, but more aesthetically sensitive builders had lately prevailed, and now the place was cedar-shingled and much more acceptable by Vineyard standards. I went inside and found Sergeant Dom Agganis, wearing civvies, at his desk.

"No Sabbath crisis, please," said big Dom, raising his hands in horror. "I plan to watch the Sox this afternoon."

"The Red Sox playing on Sunday is the essence of a Sabbath crisis," I said, "but I won't get between you and your masochistic yearnings. What I'd like to know is when Matthew Duarte died."

"None of your business," said Dom, not unexpectedly.

"The ME must have come to some conclusion by now," I said. "It's been five days. I can guess that the autopsy will say that Duarte was offed by a person or persons unknown who used a gun to blow a hole in the back of his head. I'll leave the medical details to those who know what they mean, but I'd like to know when it happened. I can find out the hard way if I have to, but you can save me some time and effort."

"Why should I? You're sticking your nose in another criminal investigation where you don't belong. Go home and play with your kids." Dom was having fun.

"I don't care about your criminal investigation," I lied. "I'm just trying to track down some missing merchandise that may have passed through Duarte's hands. It would help me to know when Duarte got croaked."

"Oh, yeah? How would it help?"

"People move around. His wife was supposedly over on Nantucket when it happened, for instance, but if I don't know when Duarte got hit I can't be sure that she really wasn't there when the gun went off. Like that."

"What's that got to do with your missing merchandise?" He glanced at a sheet of paper on the desk. "By which I presume you mean those soapstone birds your friend Mahsimba told me about."

"I haven't known Mahsimba long enough to know whether he's a friend, but, yeah, those birds. There may be a link between Duarte's death and the birds, and I may be getting close to it."

Dom looked a little less bored. "Oh? What makes you think so?"

"Because somebody took a shot at me."

He immediately became serious. "Tell me."

I did, then handed him the slug. "This is the bee that tried to sting me."

He looked at it, then put it in a small plastic bag and placed the bag in a drawer of his desk. "And you figure it's because somebody doesn't like you nosing around. What do you know that makes you dangerous?"

I shook my head. "Nothing you probably don't know. Daniel Duarte, Matthew's father, was involved with the sale of the birds. Last year sometime a guy named Brownington interviewed him, trying to trace the sale. Supposedly Duarte wouldn't name the buyer, but Brownington learned that Matthew may have been the sales agent. A little later the old man was killed in a car crash and Brownington disappeared."

"Automobile accidents happen all the time."

"Brownington was working for an outfit that's suspected of trafficking in stolen artifacts. They think the birds belong to them, and hired Brownington to get them back. Brownington used to work for Interpol and knows the way to play rough games. Maybe Duarte *père* died accidentally, but if he didn't it might not be a surprise if there's also a link between his death and Matthew's and the sale of the birds."

"And you've been rounding up the usual suspects, or something like that."

"I'd like to know who didn't do it."

"And I'd like to know what you know or think you know."

I spread my hands. "I'm an open book. Ask and it shall be revealed to you."

"Stay here." He went out of the office and down the hall and came back with two cups of coffee. "Now, start at the beginning and we'll go over the whole thing again."

So I did that, giving him most of the facts and some of my conjectures. I told him about Joe Begay's help, but I didn't mention my excursion into Duarte's barn or what I saw and thought there. He listened and occasionally asked a question. When I was through, our cups were empty.

Agganis thought for a while, then said, "I hope your delicate feelings won't be hurt if I tell you that Mahsimba already told me most of this."

"That was smart, I think. Anyway, now that I've shown you my soul, you can tell me when Matthew Duarte was shot."

"You're going to have to introduce me to your pal Begay. He sounds like a useful guy to know."

"I'll invite you the next time Joe and I have high tea. Are you going to tell me or not?"

"Don't get in a snit, but do go home and stay out of this business. I don't want the next homicide to be yours."

"I'm not in a snit. If you don't tell me, I'll just go home and call my pal Quinn, up at the *Globe*, in Boston. He'll get his hands on the ME's report and tell me what I want to know and I'll tell him there's a good story down here about the police not solving yet another murder on the Vineyard. He likes stories about incompetent cops on islands oozing with money."

"One of those 'Killer Stalks Homes and Byways

of Xanadu While Police Flounder' stories, I imagine. The fact that we're not floundering won't make any difference, of course."

"Of course not. The chamber of commerce will have a tizzy, and Quinn will be in reporter's heaven."

He glanced at his watch. "You want to watch the game with me?"

"No. I've got problems enough without watching the Sox kick the ball around." I got up. "See you later."

"Stay in touch."

"Sure."

"By the way, Duarte got himself shot early Tuesday morning. Six A.M. or so. That's about seven or eight hours before you found him. Nobody we've talked to, including the neighbors, saw anything or heard anything, but we're still asking questions. Maybe somebody driving by saw a car going in or coming out. We're putting a notice in the local papers asking for any help we can get. We may learn something."

It's not easy to get away with murder, but if you're just a little lucky and don't feel proud or guilty, you can sometimes manage it.

"While you're feeling talkative, have you had any luck IDing the Horseman?"

"I hear that there are Brownington family blood samples in Boston. DNA may do the job, but I don't have any results yet. Brownington was a very smart, very tough guy, according to Mahsimba. How would a guy like that manage to get himself killed so fast here on our little island?"

"Even smart, tough guys get killed," I said.

"You got any suspects in mind for that job?"

"Somebody smarter and tougher."

"Get out of here. And be careful."

I got.

It was another lovely day, and I was in a shellfishing mood, so I went home and put a couple of quahog rakes on the roof rack beside the fishing rods (because you never go to the beach without your rods, even if you don't plan to fish) and stuck rubber gloves and clam baskets in the back of the truck.

Inside the house I invited anyone who wanted to go to join me on the flats, with the option of sitting on the beach while I hunted clams. I got three volunteers and a suggestion that didn't surprise me.

"Maybe John and Mattie and Mahsimba would like to join us," said Zee. "Where are we going?"

"I had the far corner of Katama Bay in mind," I said. "The tide should be about right. Give Mattie a call and have them meet us there. We won't be hard to find."

There was a scramble for bathing suits and beach gear while Zee made her telephone call, then the fast preparation of a lunch basket, and we were off, rattling to the island's south shore. There we headed east behind parked Jeeps whose owners were enjoying one of their last Sundays on Norton's Point Beach, before the environmentalists closed it down for the summer.

At the Chappy end of Katama Bay there are sand flats that reach out into the bay and provide homes to both soft-shell clams and quahogs. When the tide is right, the place is covered with diggers and rakers. Today the tide was right and we were not the first ones there. Still, there were clams enough for all, so as Zee and the kids unpacked the truck and laid out the beach gear, I took my favorite basket and rake and walked out to the warm, shallow waters of the quahog grounds.

As I walked I wasn't thinking of shellfish.

25

With the warm June sun beating down on my naked back, and the placid water lapping comfortably against my thighs, I raked in circles, moving slowly from place to place, seeking quahog city, where the innocent clams would be waiting, unaware of the brevity of their futures. As, no doubt, Matthew Duarte had been unaware almost a week earlier at 6 A.M.

To the north, this side of the narrows, and to the west, along the shore of Katama Point, boats were anchored. Out beyond the flats, where the water was deep enough for a keel or centerboard, a pair of small sloops sailed slowly through the gentle southwest wind.

Between me and the shore where I'd left Zee and the kids, people were on the flats digging holes and enjoying the sun on their backs. There were little children side by side with their elders, for there was no water deep enough to be a danger to them. As I looked back that way, I saw that John Skye's Jeep had arrived.

I moved farther out, raking lazy circles and picking up a stray quahog here and there before going on and raking yet another circle. I was in no hurry, so the hunting was as good as the finding.

When next I looked back I saw Zee leading Mahsimba out onto the flats to teach him how to dig for steamers. I didn't know if people went clamming in Zimbabwe, but it was a skill that Mahsimba might one day find valuable if, say, he was ever cast away on a desert island surrounded by clams. Or if he lived on Martha's Vineyard.

I put my imaginings about Mahsimba aside and continued thinking about what I'd observed and heard over the past week.

Miguel Periera had, it seemed, outgrown his youthful inclinations to live the rowdy life, and was settled into being a family man with a profitable career of catering to the gastronomical whims of the island's wealthy citizens. He was apparently a classic example of what crime statistics clearly illustrated: that many a young hooligan finally grows up and abandons his or her wild ways. A city swept by crime slowly becomes more sedate as a generation of outlaw youth matures, and only becomes violent again when the next generation of hoodlums-to-be reaches its teens and takes to the life of turmoil and danger until its survivors grow older in their turn and the cycle is repeated.

Of course, not all young criminals abandon the life. Some go on to become middle-aged or even old thieves and killers. I'd read more than once of men in their eighties still robbing banks or murdering their enemies.

Rose Abrams, on the other hand, had never been a wild island girl, but rather a more or less conventional local woman who, though unmarried to Miguel, constituted the family he now enjoyed. She worked part-time for Charles Mauch and had done the same for Matthew Duarte, and had apparently made herself into a valuable and sophisticated assistant for each of them, even to the point of being accepted into the parlors of the wealthiest members of the island's artistic community. Not bad progress for a Vineyard girl with no money and a limited artistic education.

I thought of her collapse at the news of Matthew Duarte's death and of Charles Mauch's cool response to the same news. Mauch interested me. He was rich, highly educated, aesthetically sensitive, well traveled, and of almost legendary stature as a scholar. Gerald Jenkins had less money and less international stature but was otherwise much the same sort of person. Except that he carried a pistol.

How many other pistol packers were there among the aesthetically elite? Had one of them put the bullets into Matthew Duarte's brain and the Headless Horseman's heart?

I thought about Georgie Hall and wondered if she had cause to wax Matthew. She didn't seem the type, but maybe her husband was. You usually don't make the big bucks and keep them by being a wimp. Brent Hall hadn't gotten to the top of the ladder without being willing to step on at least a few fingers or faces. Had Brent found Georgie and Matthew in a relationship closer than art dealer and client, and decided to end it the old-fashioned way? Where had Brent been when Matthew had bought it? Did that make any difference, since Brent was rich enough to hire someone else to do his dirty work?

Maybe, because for most amateurs and even for most professional criminals, it's not easy to find a hired killer when you need one. You have to ask people to identify one for you, and hope they won't tell anyone else that you inquired, and you have to keep asking until you finally find somebody who claims to actually know such a killer, then you have to meet the supposed killer and make the financial arrangements, then you have to hope that everything goes right and that nobody will brag or get drunk and talk to the wrong listener, and that your supposed killer for hire isn't really a cop wearing a wire, etc., etc.

It might be easier and safer just to do the job yourself.

That would probably be as true for Brent Hall as for anyone else.

I considered Sam Hopewell. Did he and Matt have a falling-out over some business matter or over Matthew's impending divorce from Connie? Or was it possible that Sam was going to benefit from Matthew's death? Matthew's widow would probably inherit her husband's business, and what if Sam and Connie were hot and heavy and planned to hitch their wagons to a common star after a respectable period of grieving for the deceased?

I realized that I had hooked Matthew up to almost every woman I'd met in the past week except to his own wife. Extramarital relationships were much on my mind.

The classic motives for violent crime are sex, money, power, and fear, usually in some mixture. I doubted if Matthew's death was anything more esoteric.

I looked behind me. There, a hundred yards away, Zee and Mahsimba were side by side on their knees, digging for clams. I thought I could see laughter on their faces. They looked like Adam and Eve. Joshua and Diana were digging small holes near them. You're never too young to learn how to clam.

I felt my rake strike what was surely a quahog and pressed my fingers down on the handle to get the teeth under the clam as I pulled the rake toward me. As I pulled, I felt another hit, then another. Clam city at last. When I brought the rake up, there were four littlenecks in it. I rinsed off the mud and sand and dropped them into my basket.

I raked a new circle and brought up various sized quahogs on almost every pull: littlenecks, cherrystones, and growlers for chowder. I raked the circle clean and walked out farther. Another circle full of clams. I felt the sun grow hotter on my shoulders as I filled my basket. When it was well rounded, I walked back toward shore, passing happy diggers and coming finally to my family and Mahsimba.

The kids came running.

"Wow, Pa. You got a lot of quahogs!"

"Enough for today. How are you guys doing?"

"We got some steamers. Come and see!"

I went and saw. There were a dozen steamers in the kids' basket and a lot more in the one beside Zee and Mahsimba, who sat back on their heels as I came up. Their legs and gloved hands were muddy. They looked happy.

"What do you think?" asked Zee. "Do we have enough for a clambake? I've been telling Mahsimba about classic New England clambakes and that we should have one before he has to go home."

I looked at Mahsimba. "Do you have to go home?"

He nodded. "When my work here is done, I may go to California before returning to my country, but certainly I will be going."

"How do you like clamming?"

He glanced at his muddy rubber gloves, then at

Zee, and then looked up at me. "I've had a good instructor. It is always interesting to learn what people will eat."

"There's a lot of speculation about the first person who ever ate an oyster," I said, "and I once read about warriors in Mongolia who lived by opening veins in the necks of their horses and drinking the warm blood. Not enough to harm the horses, but enough to sustain the riders."

"Perhaps if you visit Zimbabwe I can show Zee and you how to find and prepare some of the insects and rodents that my people believe are fine foods indeed."

"I'd love to see Africa," said Zee.

"It is the most varied and beautiful continent on earth," said Mahsimba. "Only a fool would not love Africa."

"Before eating these clams," I said, "we'll put them in a bucket of salt water overnight so they can spit out the sand in their systems. By tomorrow night they'll be ready. Come to a clambake at our house and you can take the memory home with you. I'll invite John and Mattie and the twins, too. Between your steamers and my quahogs, we'll have plenty to eat."

His golden eyes left mine and joined Zee's. "If it is not an imposition, I would be pleased to accept."

"It's not an imposition," I said before Zee could reply, and I walked on toward the beach, where John and Mattie were stretched out absorbing the beneficial rays of the sun.

"Nice catch," said Mattie, opening an eye and closing it again.

"You two and the girls are invited to a Jackson clambake tomorrow night," I said.

"We accept," said John. "I'll do the dishes afterward."

"We'll be using paper plates."

"That's why I volunteered."

"That's what I thought."

I put the rake on the roof rack, the clam basket in the shade of the car, and stretched out on the old bedspread that served us as a beach blanket.

I adjusted a rolled towel under my head for a pillow, tipped the bill of my cap over my eyes, and let the sun improve my early-summer belly tan while it burned the poisons from my psyche. In time it sealed the bottle holding the genie of jealousy and I was able to think about Periera Food Service.

26

We came home from the beach in midafternoon, where, after filling a couple of five-gallon buckets with salt water and depositing our clams therein, I showered then checked the phone book for the address of Periera Food Service, which, I discovered, was the same as Miguel's home address. I'd known the business was located up in Vineyard Haven someplace, but I had never been there. There are a lot of places on Martha's Vineyard that I've never seen and probably never will.

While Zee and the kids were climbing into clean clothes, I put my pistol in my belt and pulled my shirt down over the butt. I announced that I'd be back in an hour or so, and drove to Vineyard Haven. I figured that Miguel would either be resting at home or working in the office, so either way I had a good chance of finding him.

Unless he devoted the Sabbath to meditation and prayer in church, which I doubted, since even in his maturity he was not known for his spirituality. No, he was the same sensual, emotional person he'd always been, although he now had those inclinations under control. Few of us change our fundamental character; we can only change its form.

Rose Abrams had managed that. From being the

pretty, passionate, intuitive, sometimes intellectually unsure girl I had dated long ago, she had become a handsome woman who had trained her mind to be as powerful as her feelings. That combination of intellect, intuition, and emotion had allowed her to overcome the limitations of her upbringing and to become a member of the Vineyard art world.

That she and Miguel had become a couple was not surprising since both were onetime social misfits who had climbed out of their unpromising pasts and into a present that was filled with ambition. Both were doing well in their professional lives; both were handsome and full of life, and seemed set upon a path of success.

But few lives are as idyllic as they may seem to others, and where emotions run deep, dangers are double. Our feelings can carry us away like the tornado carried Dorothy to Oz, and we can find ourselves in a world of passions we thought existed only in the imaginations of poets.

The office of Periera Food Service was in a separate building next to Miguel and Rose's house. The house was classic Vineyard: a medium-sized Cape sheathed in weathered cedar shingles and gray-painted window and door frames. The yard behind the white picket fence was neatly kept, with a closely mowed lawn and flower beds, and there was a two-car garage on the side of the house opposite the office. All in all, the place had the look of prosperous middle-class owners, which was probably just what Miguel, and perhaps Rose, aspired to be.

I parked in front of the office and went to the door. It was locked, but beside a buzzer there was a sign informing me that if no one was in the office, a ring of the bell between the hours of eight to five would bring someone from the house.

I put my finger to the buzzer and a minute later Rose Abrams came out of the house. I hadn't seen her since I'd first gone to Mauch's house. She looked gaunt, but there was a forced smile on her face until she saw who was waiting for her. Then the smile faded a bit.

"J.W., is that you?"

"I'm not a customer, I just want to talk. How are you feeling?"

She had a key that she put in the door lock. "I'm fine, thank you. The other day, I was . . . It was just such a shock to hear about Matthew." She opened the door. "Please, come in. What is it you want to talk about?"

"Business must be booming for you."

She nodded. "Miguel is doing very well."

"I had no idea a business like this could be so profitable."

"He works hard."

"I saw him up-island last week. He was delivering one order to Mrs. Hall and picking up another one at the same time."

Again the dull nod. "Yes, he often takes orders while making deliveries. A lot of our customers take deliveries every week."

"I know you work most of the week, but do you ever go off-island with Miguel? It seems like it would be a nice break for you."

She rubbed her forehead. "Oh, once in a while. Not often. Sometimes Miguel's schedule is just too hectic for me to go along. I'd just be in the way. I do go off with him. Not often, but sometimes."

"Did you ever do extra work for Charles Mauch or Matthew Duarte?"

She stared at me. "What do you mean?"

"I mean you worked for them but did you ever put in extra time? Long days, evenings, that sort of thing."

She looked away, then back. "Sometimes when things get busy they've needed some extra help. And I could always use the money."

She seemed emotionally frail, I thought, so I leaned forward and used a firm voice. "Were you and Matthew Duarte lovers?"

She paled. "Of course not. How cruel of you. Think of poor Connie."

She was right about the cruelty, but I kept using it. "Connie Duarte might have been shocked about Matthew's death, but she wouldn't be shocked about you and him. Matthew told Sam Hopewell he was leaving her for you, and the word got at least as far as Barbara Butters, who told me. Unless Connie was a complete fool, she knew what was going on."

"Stop it! You don't know what you're talking about!"

But she didn't leap to her feet or slap my face or otherwise manifest outraged innocence. She sat there with tears welling in her eyes.

"You worked with him. He was handsome and rich and he liked women. I saw how the news of his death affected you. You two were lovers and he was going to leave Connie and marry you, isn't that right?"

"Please, don't shout at me."

I hadn't been shouting. I studied her. "That was the plan, wasn't it?"

Tears poured from her eyes and words from her

mouth. "Yes. Yes! Why are you doing this to me? What difference does it make now? Matt's dead. My God, why can't you just leave me alone? You don't know how I feel! You never loved anybody. You're cold and cruel. Go away! Leave me alone!"

But I didn't go away. I watched her weep, then got up and walked behind her chair and put my hands on her shoulders and began to knead the tight muscles there. After a time, the shaking of her body began to ease.

"I'm sorry," I said, "but I had to be absolutely sure."

She said nothing.

"Did Miguel know about you and Matthew Duarte?"

She nodded and rubbed at her eyes. "He knew. He and I have been slipping apart. When we started together we were alike, but for the past year we've been growing in different directions. Neither of us wanted it to be that way, but that's the way it is. Miguel wants us to be like we were. He thinks we can be, but people change."

Some people do. Others don't.

"Is Miguel around?" I asked.

"He's in the house." Her voice was muffled.

"No, he isn't," said a voice from the doorway.

I turned and Miguel was standing there, his face wearing a vulpine smile. He walked over to the office desk and sat down.

"Does Rose know about the work you did for Matthew Duarte?" I asked. "Not the food service. The other work."

He looked at Rose. "Why don't you go up to the house, sweetheart?" he said. "Wash your face. You'll feel better. J.W. and I have to talk."

But Rose only stood up. "What other work? What other work are you talking about, Jeff?"

"I'll explain it all later," said Miguel in a soothing voice. "I have to talk with J.W. first."

"Miguel and Matthew had a deal," I said to Rose. "When Miguel took the truck to the mainland, he did more than shop for rich people who were too cheap to pay Vineyard prices. He transported illegal art objects to and from the island, and Matthew paid him good money to do it. That's why Periera Food Service is doing so well. It's got an income that has nothing to do with food. It's also the reason he probably wasn't eager to take you with him even on your days off from work. Isn't that right, Miguel?"

"I don't know what you're talking about."

"I found records in the barn for deliveries from FedEx, UPS, and other shippers. They looked legit enough, but Periera Food Service was listed there, too, and that didn't make sense if food was what you were delivering, since food would have been delivered to the house, not the barn. Ergo, you were delivering or picking up business merchandise, and it was probably illicit stuff because it was safer to have you do it than to have legal outfits handle it. You were an ideal carrier because you had legitimate reasons to come and go all the time. Even in the winter when there weren't as many rich food-and-drink customers on the island, you could still justify one trip a week to America."

"I never asked about what was in the crates," said Miguel with a shrug. "I don't know anything about art, one way or another. I just drive a truck. Rose, honey, please leave us alone for a few minutes."

"No. How long have you been doing this, Miguel?"

"It's just some business you never knew about," said Miguel. "Go to the house."

"I'm not a cop," I said to him, "so I don't really care whether or not you and Matthew Duarte were in the art-smuggling racket. I'm only interested in whether you transported a couple of stone birds, and where you transported them."

His left hand was on the desk, but the right was out of sight. "I can't help you," he said.

I thought he was lying. I said, "A guy named David Brownington came by looking for them about six months ago."

Miguel shook his head. "Never heard of him."

But Rose had. "I remember him. He had an English accent. I was just getting ready to leave the office when he came in. He and Matthew were talking when I left."

Things were coming together. "Did you see him again?"

She shook her head. "No. No, only that once. Matthew said later that he thought he'd left the island. Who is he? What are these birds you're talking about?"

"Miguel here can probably verify that Brownington never left the island. At least, not all of him. Isn't that right, Miguel?"

"You're spinning this yarn, J.W."

I looked at Rose. "Do you remember what else happened just after Brownington was here? They found the Headless Horseman by the bridal path. Right now, even as we speak, up in Boston they're testing some DNA evidence that may identify the body. My bet is that it's Brownington."

Her face was full of confusion. "I don't understand."

I told her about Brownington and the birds and about Daniel Duarte's supposed auto accident in California.

"Then Brownington came here to muscle Matthew," I said. "For leverage, he probably mentioned the old man's 'accident.' That might normally have been a good idea but in this case, it wasn't, because Brownington got careless and Matthew, or maybe Miguel here, killed him. How am I doing, Miguel?"

Miguel's face was intent. "I had nothing to do with Brownington's death."

"But you had something to do with getting rid of his head and hands, didn't you? It's not easy to get rid of a whole body, but the head and hands and clothes can be boxed or bagged up pretty easily and dropped off in some rubbish container in America. And without prints or a face, a naked corpse is hard to identify."

Miguel said nothing, but his eyes were bright and thoughtful.

"I have another theory, too," I said. "You may not have killed Brownington, but I think you may have killed Matthew Duarte."

Hearing those words, Rose made a choking sound that drew my eyes to her as I reached for my revolver. But Miguel was quicker than I expected. When I looked back at him there was already a pistol in his hand. It was pointed at me.

27

"Put your hands up in the air," said Miguel. "That's right. Just like in the movies. Rose, walk around behind him and see if he has any weapons."

She stared at him. "Miguel, what are you doing?"

"Trust me," he said. "Just do what I say. I'll explain everything."

"I'll bet you will," I said. The muzzle of his pistol looked like the entrance to a tunnel.

"Shut up. Rose, do what I say. He may be armed. He's a dangerous man."

Rose hesitated.

"I think he killed Matthew," said Miguel. "And he may have killed Brownington. Do as I say, or he may kill us, too."

Rose's eyes grew wide. She sidled around behind me.

"Be careful," said Miguel.

Rose's hands floated around my waist and took the revolver from my belt.

Miguel's voice was that of a hypnotist. "That's good, darling. Now step away from him and come over here. Then we can call the police."

Rose walked to the desk. Her face was full of fear.

"Good," he said. He rose and came around to the front of the desk. "Now we don't have to worry about him hurting us."

"Two guns to none makes that pretty sure," I said.

"Shut up," said Miguel.

"I don't think Miguel's going to call the police," I said to Rose. "I think you should do it yourself. Right now."

"No, don't do that," said Miguel. "I have a better idea. I'll take him to them myself."

I shook my head. "No, you won't. I'll wait right here." I looked at Rose. "Your boyfriend here has already killed at least one man, and if he gets me alone in his car, I'll be shot trying to escape, sure as the world. Isn't that right, Miguel?"

"I've never killed anyone," said Miguel. "I may have hauled some freight for Matthew and I may have trucked those birds up to Mauch after he bought them, but that's all I ever did. Rose, honey, there's some duct tape over on that shelf. Bring it here. We'll bundle J.W. up so he can't cause a fuss."

My mouth felt like the Gobi Desert. I said, "Call the cops, Rose. If you let this guy take me out of here it'll be the last time you see me alive."

"Shut your mouth!" Miguel's voice was commanding. "Rose, get that tape!"

"I don't know what I should do." Rose's eyes were wide and her hands were twisting each other.

"Just bring me the tape, sweetheart. This man is a killer and we have to tie him up so he can't hurt anyone else."

She went to the shelf and returned with the tape. He took it. "I'm going to tie him up. If he tries to escape or hurt me, shoot him!"

My arms were aching. "It's going to be harder for you this time," I said to Miguel. "You've got a witness and I don't plan on turning my back on you like

Matthew did." I flicked a glance at Rose. "Miguel probably used this very pistol to kill Matthew and take a shot at me. It was you who put that hole in my windshield and blew Matthew away, isn't that right, Miguel?"

His face filled with anger and frustration. "Don't believe a word of it, Rose! J.W. killed Matthew and now he's trying to turn you against me!" He lifted the pistol. "You shut your lying mouth or I'll shut it for you!"

I knew I was going to die, and in that surety all my fear was suddenly gone, but my voice sounded far away, as though it were coming from another room.

"I didn't even know Matthew," I said, speaking to Rose but watching Miguel. "But Miguel knew that Matthew was taking you away from him and he couldn't stand it. So last Tuesday, before he caught the morning boat to America, he went to Matthew's house. He knew Matthew would be alone because Connie was over on Nantucket. He shot Matthew and then went about his normal business.

"It's getting easier, isn't it, Miguel? First you make a deal with Matthew to transport illegal goods, then you go another step and help him out by using your refrigerated truck to haul Brownington's head and hands off to some Dumpster in America, then you kill Matthew, and now you're going to have another crack at killing me. And when you finish with me, are you going to kill Rose, too? You were slime as a kid and you're still slime."

Miguel pointed the pistol at my head. His voice was tight. "I warned Matthew. I told him to break off from Rose, but he just laughed, and now I've warned you but you won't shut your mouth either. Well, I stopped his laugh and I'm stopping your talk." With perfect clarity I watched his finger tighten on the trigger.

They say you never hear the shot that kills you. Could be, although there are, no doubt, plenty of exceptions to the rule. Whether Miguel heard the one that killed him I'll never know, because he didn't say a word about it but simply plunged forward onto the floor, probably dead before he hit it. His pistol did go off, but the bullet went into a wall and not into me.

I let my aching arms fall and looked at Rose, who was holding my revolver in both of her hands and looking dazedly down at Miguel's body.

I stepped around the body and took the pistol from her and put it on the desk.

"Thank you," I said. "You saved my life."

"He really was going to kill you, wasn't he?"

"Yes. He was desperate and wasn't thinking clearly."

"He killed Matthew because of me?"

"You were leaving him, and he blamed Matthew. I think he might have shot you next, then himself. It's a common pattern."

"My God! I can't believe it." She sagged, and I put her in a chair before calling the police.

Sergeant Dom Agganis, having taken my statement, clicked off the tape recorder on his desk, and our conversation became informal.

"I thought I asked you not to bring me any Sabbath crises."

"I figured the ball game was over by the time I went up to see Miguel. Who won?"

"Pedro mowed them down. Too bad the Sox don't have another pitcher."

"They need Pedro and four days of rain."

"You're going to succeed in getting yourself killed someday," he said. "You know that."

"No, I'm not. I'm giving up this investigating business for good. It's back to surf casting for me."

"The Wild East is wilder than the Wild West, you know."

"Yeah, yeah."

"Speaking of the Wild West, tell me again about that six-shooter up-island."

"It's in Brent Hall's den, hanging on a wall. A forty-one-caliber Colt, model 1889. Matthew Duarte sold it to Georgie Hall as a weapon that once belonged to Jesse James. But that was a lie because Jesse James was killed in 1882. My guess is that it's the gun that killed Brownington, and that Duarte got rid of it by palming it off on Georgie, who doesn't know a thing about guns or Jesse James. If she hadn't hung that little tag on it, it probably never would have caught my eye."

"Did I tell you that the DNA results are in and that the Horseman is Brownington? Good guess on your part."

"It makes sense. Brownington probably threatened Matthew but underestimated him and Matthew dropped him. Or maybe Miguel did it. Whoever did it, Matthew knew that if the body was found and identified, it could lead the cops back to him, so he stripped him and cut off his head and hands. No clothes, no face, no fingerprints, and nobody looking for the victim. Pretty good thinking. He probably burned Brownington's ID. That's what I'd have done, at least."

"Maybe I should be taking notes so in case we get the same MO again, we can come straight to you and you can solve the crime for us."

"That might be smart, Dom. Anyway, after he kacked Brownington, Matthew had to get rid of the body and the body parts. Miguel took care of the parts and Matthew probably packed the body out into the woods on a horse. I hadn't known that Matthew was a rider until I saw that tack room in the barn. If your lab boys run tests on the saddles out there, you might even come up with some traces of bloodstains or something. A lot of people up-island are riders. Mauch is one of them, I think, because I saw horses in the pasture behind his house."

"If Matthew was alive, he could probably charge you with breaking and entering. How do you know about Jesse James? You a frontier fan?"

"Every red-blooded American male is a frontier fan. The Wild West is the great myth of America, and we can't get enough of it. That's why John Wayne is still a top-ten movie star even though he's been dead for twenty years."

"Why, sure. I'm a Wayne fan myself."

"Of course you are. The forensic people thought the bullet they found in the Horseman was a thirty-eight- or forty-caliber slug, but forty-one is close enough to cause confusion. I think you should check that pistol out. If I'm wrong, no harm done. If I'm right, you have what they call a clue in the mystery novels, and in either case, Georgie Hall will have just the sort of exciting story she loves to tell or hear."

"My contribution to island gossip, eh?" Agganis

rubbed his thick head of hair. "You do get yourself into the damnedest situations. All this because you were looking for a couple of stone birds from Africa."

"And now I know where they are. I'm sort of hoping that maybe all this shooting will encourage Mauch to fess up."

"The birds are none of my business," said Agganis. "I've got real crimes to tend to. Go home and try to stay out of trouble."

"You're late," said Zee when I got home. "The kids and I have already eaten. You should have called." She spoke in that slightly irritated tone that wives use when their husbands fail to observe common courtesies and thereby cause wifely worry.

"Sorry," I said. "Something came up."

"I'll warm a plate for you."

"I'll take a drink on the balcony first."

She saw something in my face. "I'll come up, too."

"Good. I'll tell you about my trip to Vineyard Haven."

I got myself a glass and put in ice, two green olives, and a double slug of Luksosowa, and went up to the balcony. Zee was waiting, looking out over the garden and Sengekontacket Pond toward Nantucket Sound. The light of the sinking sun cast a glow on the barrier beach between the pond and the sound, where cars were moving along the highway headed for Edgartown or Oak Bluffs.

I sipped my icy drink and then, because the story would soon be public anyway, told her about the bullet hole in my windshield and my experience at Periera Food Service.

For a while, then, there was only the sound of the

wind sighing through the trees. Finally Zee said, "I'm so glad she was there and that she had a gun."

"Me, too."

"I know what she's feeling. I'll go talk with her." She looked at me. "Do you remember telling me over and over that I'd done the right thing when I killed that terrible man, and that you could never thank me enough for saving your wife and daughter?"

"I remember. I still thank you."

"I've never been able to accept that, but I think I finally understand. I'll never be able to thank Rose enough. Never!" She looked at me, then reached for me and began to cry.

28

The next morning I phoned Charles Mauch and told him about my final encounter with Miguel Periera. He responded by expressing surprise at learning of Miguel's and Matthew Duarte's criminal activities and skepticism about the veracity of reports by such men.

"Are you denying that you possess the eagles?" I asked.

"I am denying that I possess any art objects than can be certified as belonging to someone else."

"A completely honest reply, I'm sure. I think, though, that you should give consideration to the fact that four men associated with the birds have died violently within the past year, and that agents, perhaps from law enforcement groups or perhaps from less official organizations, are still looking for them right now, right here on our beloved isle."

His voice remained cool. "What has that to do with me?"

"Perhaps nothing; perhaps very much. Please feel free to contact me or Mr. Mahsimba if you have any further thoughts on the matter." I gave him John Skye's phone number and my own and rang off.

The Boston papers duly recorded the death of Miguel Periera in their Monday editions, but even though the killing had taken place on romantic

Martha's Vineyard, the reporters hadn't known enough to make much of what initially seemed to them to be just another domestic tragedy of a girl-friend killing her lover. The Tuesday edition of the *Vineyard Gazette* had more detail, and by the end of the week, after public revelation that DNA tests had proven the Headless Horseman to be David Brown-ington, the story had gotten much bigger.

On that first Monday I'd received a call from my Boston reporter friend, Quinn, telling me he was on his way down and expected an exclusive interview with me. Quinn and I had met years before when I was on the Boston PD, and we'd remained close ever since. I told him to come ahead, and that he could stay in our guest room, where he had stayed before. I got calls from other papers and electronic-media people and told them I had no comment.

When Quinn got to the house, he gave Zee a huge kiss and said he was sure I wouldn't mind sleeping on the couch while he showed her the benefits of a relationship with a real man. She thanked him but said she was saving that long-anticipated delight until the children were grown and she could give him her full attention. He sighed.

I gave him my report of recent criminal events and a list of the names of people I thought he might want to interview.

"Ah," he said, looking at it. "Twice the usual sus-pects. This should keep me down here for at least a week!"

"Oh no! Gimme back that list!" I said, reaching for it. But he snatched it away.

Good old Quinn.

Zee took time off from work and spent some of it with Rose Abrams and the rest with me, away from John and Mattie Skye and other friends. Away from Mahsimba. She and I avoided the beaches where we were sure to meet fellow fishermen, and walked up-island along the trails of Menemsha Hills, Fulling Mill Brook, Waskosims Rock, and the other tracks through the Vineyard's beautiful wild places.

Ours was a curious relationship, somewhere between that of a long-married couple and a man and a woman discovering one another for the first time. We were cautious yet happy, careful with our feelings. Sometimes we talked, but we were often silent, as though listening to the beating of the earth's heart in hopes that its rhythm was in time with our own. Sometimes we took our children with us; mostly we went alone.

It was a kind of courting, simpler for me because loving Zee was the easiest and most natural thing I'd ever done or would ever do; harder for her because she had been swept away at first sight of Mahsimba through no effort of his nor fault of hers, but simply because the gods, seeing her weakened by self-dismay over killing a man, had cast a glamour upon her, perhaps out of kindness, knowing that loving and feeling loved can make a sick soul well again.

Toward the end of the week we were looking out toward No Man's Land from the slope of Prospect Hill. The dark blue sea was flat as a mirror and the leaves were totally still in windless air. It was warm and the sun was high in a pale blue sky that dipped toward misty horizons. Time seemed to have stopped.

"Swordfishing weather," I said.

Zee took my hand. "I've finally, really gotten over killing that man, I think. Talking with Rose helped."

"Good." Any giving person can tell you that the giver always gets more than he or she gives.

"I think I'm getting over Mahsimba, too."

"Do you want to get over him?"

"He's a wonderful man."

"Yes."

"But I don't want him between us."

"You can't just stop loving someone," I said. "Love just happens. You have no choice." I, at least, had none.

"I don't think it's love. For me, seeing him was like falling down stairs. There he was and suddenly I was picking myself up from the bottom step. I'd read about such things, but I thought it was just poets' talk. But it isn't."

"No."

"He's never done a thing to encourage me. Never touched me other than shaking my hand when we first met or accepting my arm when I took his. Never said a flirting word. But from the moment I first saw him I felt like a fifteen-year-old girl high on champagne."

"I've felt fifteen once or twice."

"Have you? I think I really was fifteen the last time I felt that way. But for a while, lately, when I thought of Mahsimba it's been as though Africa were calling to me."

"A siren song."

"Yes. I've felt like Odysseus. But I didn't have anyone to tie me to the mast so I could listen but not respond. My rope has been loving you but my crew has been me, and it's been mutinous. I wanted you to make me stay, but I knew you wouldn't."

"No."

She smiled wanly and looked up at me. "No. I know you. You'd stop anyone from hurting me, but you'd never stop me from leaving you."

"I don't own slaves."

"Sometimes a woman wants to be guarded. To feel owned."

"I'll protect you, but you have to be free to leave."

"Free to go to Africa?"

"Free to go anywhere."

"Free to go home with you?"

"That most of all."

"I love you. Do you know that?"

"Yes."

"Can you live with a wife who can become infatuated with other men?"

I said, "I don't love often or well, or stop loving easily, but I do know this: you don't have a finite amount of love that you have to divide into pieces and dole out in small portions. The more you love, the more you can love. Being infatuated with Mahsimba doesn't mean you love me less."

"I think I'm getting un-infatuated."

"Good."

"Don't you have any jealous bones in your body?"

"Let's not try to find out."

"You're a strange man, Jefferson."

"At least."

She held my hand as we walked on.

By the following weekend Quinn had sent in several stories and figured he had all the information he needed or was going to get about murder and smuggled art on Martha's Vineyard.

"The only things that are missing are an official decision about who killed Brownington, and knowing what happened to the eagles. I don't know if we'll ever get either one."

"Not all mysteries have tidy endings."

"Well, if we can't get the loose ends all knitted up, the least you can do is take me fishing before I have to go back to Boston."

"Zee will catch a fish for you if you can't catch one yourself."

"Truly manly men don't need women to catch their fish for them," said Zee, clutching his arm and batting her lashes.

"You got that right, baby," said Quinn, leering at her.

We fished East Beach and caught up with the blues just north of Leland's Point. The fish weren't thick but there were enough to keep us busy for half an hour before they went on their way. Nice seven- and eight-pounders.

"You can take home as many of these as you want," I said to Quinn. "We'll fillet them and loan you a cooler. When you get back to Boston you can feed them to your girlfriends and lie about how you caught them all."

"I wish you wouldn't talk about other women while Zee's listening," said Quinn in a theatrical whisper.

"Other women?" cried Zee. "Oh, woe, oh, woe! I thought I was the only one!"

"Damn you, Jackson," hissed Quinn. "Now you've done it. You've broken the poor girl's heart!"

At home, while Zee and Quinn drank lazy martinis on the balcony and watched the kids play with the cats in the yard below, I scaled and filleted the fish. I was putting the last of them into the fridge when the phone rang.

"This is Mahsimba," said the familiar voice. "I have just received a telephone call from Charles Mauch. He wants to see me."

I felt a little rush of emotion. "What about?"

"The Zimbabwe eagles. I thought you might want to come along."

"When?"

"Now."

"Where are you?"

"In John's study."

"I'm on my way."

I reported the call to Zee, declined Quinn's request to accompany me, said I expected to be home for supper, and drove to the Skyes' farm. Mahsimba was waiting for me on the front porch. Together we headed up-island.

"Did Mauch give you any idea about why he wanted to see you?" I asked.

"Only that it concerned the birds."

I found Mauch's driveway and stopped in front of his large house. He opened the door when we knocked and looked first at me, then at Mahsimba.

"I didn't expect Mr. Jackson."

Mahsimba's voice was gentle but firm. "I suspect that if it were not for Mr. Jackson, this meeting would not be taking place. I think it's appropriate for him to hear whatever it is that you want to tell me."

Mauch inclined his head. "As you wish. Follow me, please."

He led us into the same room where we'd talked before, but there was a difference. On an ornate table stood two soapstone stelae, each fronted by a crocodile and topped by a stone bird.

Mauch stood to one side as Mahsimba and I approached and studied the sculptures. When at last we looked at him, he spoke.

"As you see, the eagles are here."

"And were here before, no doubt," said Mahsimba.

"Yes. But things have changed since our previous meetings. Brownington is dead, two Duartes are dead, and now Miguel Periera is dead. That is a considerable number of dead men, Mr. Mahsimba."

"The deaths of Matthew Duarte and Miguel Periera really had nothing to do with the eagles, Mr. Mauch."

"Not directly, certainly. But the pattern of violence impresses me, as does the ongoing search for the eagles by people who come from far lands. People such as you, sir."

"You are in no danger from me, Mr. Mauch."

"No? But what of Mr. Brownington's successor?"

"I cannot speak for Brownington's successor."

Mauch nodded. "Precisely. I have no interest in being hunted down by secret agents. Better, I think, to separate myself publicly from these lovely, bloody birds. After due consideration, I've concluded that I should give the nation of Zimbabwe the first opportunity to purchase them."

"Indeed," said Mahsimba. "And what price do you have in mind?"

"Normally I expect to make a profit on all of my financial transactions," said Mauch, "but in hopes of improving cultural relations between our nations,

I'll part with them for what I paid." He adjusted the cuff of his shirt and named a figure that I pretended did not impress me. "My purchase of the eagles was, of course, completely legal, since the birds were exported from your nation before it was, in fact, the nation it has since become, and certainly before any laws prevented such exportation. I mention that only to indicate that I have a perfect right to sell the birds to other interested parties should your nation decline the opportunity to repossess them."

He and Mahsimba wore politic expressions.

"I will contact my employers and inform them of your offer," said Mahsimba. "I trust I may depend upon you not to enter negotiations with other parties before you hear from me?"

"You may."

"And that you will properly secure the birds until such time as an agreement may be completed?"

"I have a vault."

"Then, since time is always an important consideration in these matters, we will take our leave so I can make the necessary communications." Mahsimba paused, then added, "I may presume, of course, that these birds are the actual ones and not something less?"

Mauch spread his hands. "But of course, sir. I am an honest man. I have an international reputation to maintain."

Polite smiles were exchanged as we left.

"It seems," said Mahsimba as we drove back to Edgartown, "that my work here is essentially over. I will advise Harare to take over negotiations with Mr. Mauch, and I will return to my home and my job with Interpol. I've enjoyed my visit to your country and to your lovely island. You and your friends have been most helpful and hospitable."

"You'll be missed. But won't Crompton's people be annoyed?"

"Crompton is a professional man who will know a loss when he encounters one."

"But won't he be rather miffed at you?"

"No doubt. I'll be watching my back for a while. But then, I always watch my back. You and Zeolinda must come to Africa. My wife and I would be pleased to be your hosts. Our children are almost the same ages as yours, so your little ones, too, would have companions eager to introduce them to Zimbabwe."

"You're married?"

"To a woman as lovely as your wife. I'm more eager to see her than I can say. I increasingly dislike the travels my work requires. I envy the life you lead here, always close to your family. You're a fortunate man."

"Yes."

I got home in time for supper, and afterward went with Zee and Quinn up to the balcony with coffee and cognac.

Quinn was happy because now the only thing he didn't have was a final, official decision about who killed Brownington.

Off to our right, in the southern sky, the stars that glittered at us also glittered every night over Africa. Beneath them, half a world away, a wife was waiting for the return of her husband, and her children were wishing their father were home.

Eight hundred years earlier those same stars had shone down upon the empire of Monomotapa, where, within towering walls, an artisan in stone was carving a stele adorned with a crocodile and topped with an eagle. A thousand years in the future, long after current empires, including America, had crumbled to dust, those stars would be unchanged.

"Look!" said Zee, pointing. "There! It's a satellite!"

The tiny light moved steadily across the heavens, a man-made star moving at incredible speed. It was a marvel to match the towers of Great Zimbabwe. We watched it until it disappeared into the depths of the timeless, uncaring, and ethereally beautiful sky.

RECIPES

All Delicious

Paella à la Valenciana

J.W. adapted this recipe from a Spanish cookbook he found at a yard sale.

*1 small chicken, boiled (save 2¼ cups of the stock
   to cook rice; water must be hot)*
*8 pork sausages (chicken or turkey sausages may be
   substituted)*
½ cup olive oil
1 small onion, chopped
3 cloves garlic, finely chopped
3 tomatoes, peeled and chopped
2 green or red peppers, peeled and chopped
1 tsp. paprika
½ tsp. saffron or turmeric
Salt and pepper
1 cup of rice
6 canned artichoke hearts
½ cup peas
½ lb. cleaned shrimp

Boil the chicken and strip the meat from the bones. Cut the meat into bite-sized chunks. Save the hot water for cooking the rice.

Brown the sausages in some of the olive oil in a *large* frying pan and cut into bite-sized chunks.

In remaining olive oil, sauté the onion, garlic, tomatoes, and peppers in the same pan.

Return the sausages to the pan and add the chicken pieces and spices.

Stir in the rice and pour in the hot water.

Cook on low heat for about 15 minutes, then add artichoke hearts, peas, and shrimp.

Cook another 10 minutes, until rice is tender, and serve.

Note: There are as many kinds of paella as there are paella cooks. Substitutions for the above ingredients can be made freely. For instance, Phil Craig lately has been using hot turkey sausage in lieu of pork sausage because his wife, Shirl, doesn't eat pork.

The general idea is to cook all of the ingredients in one dish until they're done but not overdone.

Saffron is very expensive. You can substitute turmeric.

CHICKEN ENCHILADAS

One of the main differences between these chicken enchiladas and others is that J.W. uses dessert crepes instead of tortillas for wrappers.

CREPES

Combine: 2 beaten eggs, ⅔ cup milk, ⅓ cup water, ½ tsp. vanilla

Combine: ¾ cup flour, 1 tsp. baking powder, 1 tsp. salt, and 2 tbsp. powdered sugar

Pour egg mixture into flour mixture and mix until most of the lumps are gone. Place a 5- to 6-inch frying pan or crepe pan over moderate heat, add a bit of oil, and pour in just enough crepe mix to make a thin cake. Cook, turning once. Repeat. Set crepes aside.

FILLING

Slice 2 large onions and fry in 2 tbsp. butter and a bit of water until tender. Remove, drain, and mix with 2 cups of diced, cooked, skinned chicken, ½ cup chopped pimento, 8 oz. diced cream cheese, and a few shakes of hot pepper sauce. Salt to taste. (Note: Cream cheese is much easier to dice if it's frozen.)

Spoon about ⅓ cup of filling into each crepe. Roll and place crepes, seam side down, in a baking dish. Brush with milk or cream and sprinkle with 2 cups grated Jack cheese.

Bake in 375° oven for 20–25 minutes.

Garnish, if you wish, with pitted ripe olives, radishes, and coriander.

(Makes about 12 crepes)

FLAN

½ cup sugar
4 eggs
1 cup skim milk
1 tsp. vanilla
Dash of salt

Caramelize ¼ cup sugar in a small, heavy skillet and quickly pour into an 8½–inch circular baking pan, tilting pan to coat bottom as much as possible.

Mix eggs, milk, remaining ¼ cup sugar, vanilla, and salt, and pour mixture into the pan.

Set round pan in larger baking pan, fill larger pan to a depth of 1 inch with hot water, bake in a 325° oven for 30 minutes, or until a knife comes out clean when inserted into the center of the flan.

Cool pan on a wire rack, then cover and refrigerate until cold. Loosen flan from the sides of the pan, invert onto a platter, and serve.

(Makes 8 servings)